THE CHRISTMAS PRESENT

FRANCES AMATI

For Handsome and Gloria,
Who were loved too much, to be gone so soon.

ACKNOWLEDGMENTS

Someone once asked me to choose two words that described my life. I said "alone" and "surrounded." Little did I know, in that moment, that I had just described the life of a writer.

Writing can be a solitary world where the voices in your head demand enough attention that they become your primary social circle. Conversely, the world your voices tell you about can't possibly come to fruition without the tribe that surrounds you.

I have been blessed with an amazing tribe.

My son, Evan, who challenged me to take up writing as more than a hobby.

My daughters, Heather and Brenna, who always believe in me and reassure me that while I may be close to the edge, I'm not off the deep end. Yet.

My grandchildren: Dustin, who gives the best hugs in the world. Gaven, who has more talents than he realizes. Ethan, who loves more deeply than anyone I know. Sadie, whose goofy humor makes me laugh. And Evelyn, who wants to be a giraffe doctor—and will be a damn fine one.

My children's father, Kirk, without whom I wouldn't have such amazing children.

Kirk's parents, Ralph and Lana, who remember me at twenty. The young woman who sat in the corner reading a book while everyone else partied. Who inspire me at every age to believe in true love.

Maurizio, who expanded my world and believes I am capable of anything. Really.

My sisters: Pat, who calls me "punkin," and loves me to no end. Holly, who may have left this world in 2015, but never leaves my thoughts.

Lesley, who was there when I was five and has never left me. The sister of my heart.

For my fabulous writing buddies, Alexis Lusonne Montgomery and Janis Lee Thereault, who drew me into their writing group and never let me go, their inspiration and criticism always on tap. Louella Nelson, her fabulous writing classes are just the start. Debra Holland, who edited my first short story.

My boss, Linda, at my day job—because for some reason my lender thinks I should pay my mortgage every month. She thinks I'm fabulous and encourages me in my dreams—all of them.

My Irish Wolfhounds: Handsome, Aislinn, Phira, Hala and Valkyrie—who show me what love is every day.

I could ramble on forever. Because when I think about it, there is a continuous stream of love and support ranging from that person who said one kind thing that made my day to the person who said the thing that dismissed or annoyed me and made me work harder, just to prove them wrong. It all comes down to how we look at it. I pray that each of you has an endless list of acknowledgements in your life.

SYNOPSIS

HOW FAR WOULD YOU GO TO PROTECT THE ONES YOU LOVE?

Globetrotting nature photographer, Alexandria Marsh, spent the last four years secretly guarding her family from the vengeance of her powerful ex-fiancé. As the family gathers for Christmas, Al prays for a Christmas miracle because she is running out of time to find a permanent fix.

Declan Ruaidhrí gave up on Christmas miracles long ago. Now known as Chicago's golden playboy, he takes his new friend, Edin Marsh, up on an invitation to get away for the holidays to escape Chicago's husband-hunting socialites.

The Marsh Christmas celebration brings more than family together and when long held secrets are revealed Al and

Declan team up, despite an escalating attraction they both try to deny, to keep the family safe. To fix the present they'll have to unravel the past.

Can love unwrap the present before it is too late?

CHAPTER ONE

Holiday travelers stuffed the international terminal at Chicago's O'Hare International Airport to its glass and steel gills. Cold blue columns and rows of "you could be at any airport in the world" gray leather seats contrasted sharply with the abundance of heated passengers clamoring at gate agents about flight delays and cancellations. Frustrated travelers trying to find their way home jockeyed for position with happy vacationers in Hawaiian shirts counting down to their escape from winter. Every corner of the terminal brimmed and bustled with people and activity.

Alexandria Marsh glanced at the departure board to confirm her flight was still on time and settled in for the short wait until boarding. She was *definitely* not looking forward to this trip. Christmas was snow and icicles, the scents of pine and cinnamon—not sand in your shorts, palm trees, or piña coladas. Who in their right mind celebrated Christmas in flip flops on a tropical island with ninety-degree weather? Pure logic argued that not everyone related snow to Christmas, but she tossed the logic out, retreating to her vision of the season.

Her fingers restlessly flicked the tag on her carry-on bag, the rhythmic clicking in cadence with her restless heart. *Who am I kidding? It doesn't matter where I celebrate Christmas, if my heart isn't there.* Her stomach flipped and she ceased all motion, staring at her hand resting on her bag. *I'm going to see them. It's been so long. What do I say? I can't, won't, lie. But I can't tell them the truth.* Bile, bitter in her throat, threatened to choke her and she swallowed hard. *God, if it weren't for Brent, I would just be going home for Christmas.*

She wanted to close her eyes for a moment and lose herself in a calm black darkness, but her restless energy would have none of it. Her gaze prowled the crowded terminal to settle on a harried young mother trying to corral toddler twin girls dead set on going in opposite directions. Watching their antics diverted Alexandria's underlying anxiety.

Pigtails swinging, one little girl made a break for the opposite gate. As their mother went after the runaway twin, the second turned to bolt and caught the tip of her shoe on the transition between the carpet and tile.

In one quick motion Alexandria rocked forward, scooping the little girl up before she face-planted, rising to stand with the startled youngster tucked in her arms. "Hey there, little one. You'll mess up your pretty outfit if you fall on the dirty floor."

Big blue eyes widened even farther as they rose to her face.

Alexandria figured she had about two point five seconds before fear overcame surprise and the kid started screaming. She turned toward the mother who hurried forward her with a squirming, squealing child wrapped in her arms.

"Oh, my goodness, thank you." A shaking hand pushed blonde bangs back from her face. "I'm so sorry. I just can't seem to wear them out today."

The corner of Alexandria's mouth quirked up and she rubbed the little girl's back with a gentle hand. "That's alright. I was probably worse than both of them when I was their age. I just wasn't capable of moving in two different directions. Although my mom would have likely argued that point."

The blonde cocked her head to listen as a strident voice announced pre-boarding for a flight to London. The woman grinned. "That's us. I better get them on the plane before United figures out they should leave us behind."

Alexandria smoothed the tip of her index finger over the smiling child's cheek. "You be good for your mama. You don't want Santa to have to put you on the naughty list."

Both girl's eyes went wide, and their mouths fell open. Their mother chuckled. She set the momentarily still child in her arms down and firmly took her hand.

Alexandria stood the other twin on her feet but didn't let go until her mother secured the little girl's hand with a solid grip. She smiled at the woman. "Have a safe flight and a Merry Christmas."

"Same to you. And thank you again."

As she watched them make their way to the gate, Alexandria settled back into her seat. Absently, her hand rose to gently rub away the sudden tension over her heart. *I want my own family.*

Outside the wall of windows, Chicago's winter weather battered at the glass, reminding her that a six-foot Christmas tree decorated with all her favorite things was sitting at home in Manitowoc, watching Lake Michigan alone. Sighing, she scanned the crowded terminal. She could feel someone watching her.

Across the way, a cute guy was checking her out. As his eyes met the coolness in hers, his regard slid away.

The feeling of being watched didn't dissipate and she continued to peruse the crowded terminal, drawn magnetically to six-foot-three of jaw dropping male leaning against a column. A barely-there scruff of a beard shadowed his strong, square jawline, accenting his tan. Wavy hair so dark brown it seemed black was combed back off his face, but one rebellious lock determinedly brushed his forehead. Brows, dark slashes, narrowed in focus over piercing gunmetal blue eyes that settled on her. His full lips quirked in a half-smile as he caught her gaze. His interest swept her like a hot Saharan wind.

This time, Alexandria glanced away. She leaned over, exhaling a whoosh of air as she concentrated on the camera case at her feet. In an attempt to gather her wits, she fiddled with the latches. She ventured a peek in his direction.

He still leaned against the column, staring at her with his hungry blue-gray eyes.

The term sex god popped into her head and Alexandria pushed it away. She'd learned the hard way that handsome guys like him were nothing but trouble and heartache. They were a dime a dozen--guys who thought they were God's gift to the world and the women in it were theirs for the taking. Brent had been like that.

But wait, she'd *never* actually seen a guy as heart stopping hot as this intense stranger. If other guys were nothing but trouble and heartache, what was he? She didn't think a Richter scale existed to measure him.

One more peek, just to confirm. Yeah, still watching and

still gorgeous. Like a Bokeh photo effect, her vision fixated on him while everything around him blurred.

He wasn't lean; that seemed too tame a description. His was a predator's body.

A pang of envy flashed for the charcoal gray sweater hugging his strong broad shoulders, molding his chest, and the well-worn jeans encasing his long powerful legs and hips. As an unbidden vision of him naked under a waterfall played on the high def screen in her mind, her cheeks grew warm. She blinked long and slow to clear her thoughts.

His regard was as hard as the body controlling it and still focused on her.

A voice announced the boarding for her flight. Thanking the heavens she stood abruptly and, with an uncharacteristic lack of coordination, snatched up her camera case and bag and headed for the gate agent like she was being chased by a pack of wolves.

The abrupt departure of the tall, long-legged redhead put a slight smile on Declan Ruaidhrí's face. At least, she was on his flight. Her luminous emerald eyes had widened briefly in sexual awareness of him before her gaze slid away. He had been all too mindful of her discreet scrutiny; the hardening in his groin was evidence enough of that.

Declan was a bit baffled by her aversion. Most women made every effort to catch his eye and anything else he was willing to offer if given half the chance. She wasn't wearing a wedding ring, so the mystery of her escape excited the hunter in him, and he was definitely up for the challenge. If nothing else, he could use the diversion before he was land-locked for two weeks on a tiny island with his pal, Edin and a handful of his relatives. When Edin had handed him tickets and the promise of relaxation in paradise, it seemed like the perfect getaway.

Besides, nothing else pressed him for attention at the moment. Declan's efforts to reorganize his firm's leadership were finally opening up his time. He understood why his dad had thrust the reins of the family's pharmaceutical domain into his hands. But knowing didn't make it easier to accept.

Finding the cure was always the elusive treasure at the end of the rainbow that drew him again and again to field research. The recent years of imposed leadership were draining. Just knowing he was heading back into the field energized him. Declan's expedition manager, Hank, just needed to confirm the details of their journey. His last email indicated he didn't anticipate getting the team finalized until after New Year's.

Picking up his travel duffel, he adjusted the backpack hanging from one shoulder and made his way toward the gate. At least, no husband-hunting predators would be on hand to complicate matters. Why women seemed to think he would marry was beyond him—he would **never** allow that noose to be slipped around his neck.

He just wanted to relax for a while. As far as he knew, only Edin's girlfriend, his dad, his stepmother, and the mysterious sister, whom Edin never discussed, were going to be on hand.

Head down, the gate agent was processing passengers like a robotic checkpoint.

He handed her his boarding pass.

Concentrating on her scanning, she took it from him with a practiced hand. As she handed it back, she deigned to look at him. Interest sparked in her eyes and she nearly purred, "Welcome aboard, Mr. Roo-id-ri."

He made a brief nod of acknowledgment and strode away. The usual irritation flushed over him. Just once, he'd like a woman to actually see *him*. He avoided looking at the attendant standing guard near the flight deck and made his way toward his seat. He tossed his duffel into the overhead bin and looked down at his seat. As he regarded the back of his target's red head, his frustration fled. This was going to be fun.

———

"Excuse me, miss. I believe you are in my seat."

The strong male voice with an odd accent she couldn't place brought Alexandria's head up with a start. Her mouth opened in denial, but as she looked into his amused eyes, the words died on her lips, her text message as forgotten as the phone sitting on her lap. She'd seen that gleam of anticipation before--both an anaconda in Guyana and a tiger on the Siberian taiga looked at her with "dinner" in their eyes. She'd escaped and would do the same now.

The mystery man from the gate area stared down at her, blocking the aisle. As other passengers started to build up behind him, he stood completely at ease.

Regrouping with effort, she smiled. "I'm sorry, you must be mistaken. This is 11K and that's my seat assignment."

Mr. Hottie glanced at his boarding pass. "Well, darling, unless you want to sit on my lap all the way to Tokyo, we have an issue."

The passenger backup was starting to create a flap, and she could see the flight attendant working her way towards them.

With a grin, he held out his boarding pass. "I'll show you mine if you show me yours."

11K. Alexandria examined his pass while she pulled hers from the seatback pocket. This was going to be an issue. She knew she was in the right seat. His knowing smile irritated her. What was it with handsome men? Were they genetically programmed to be annoying to compensate for being attractive?

The bleached blonde attendant arrived. "Is there a problem, sir? We need everyone to take their seats so we can finish boarding." She sidled a little closer.

He handed her his boarding pass.

Without hesitation, the attendant turned to her. "Miss, you are in the wrong seat," she said in an irritated tone. "I need you to move to your correct seat."

The attendant's attitude sparked the inherent temper that Alexandria worked so hard to control and it flashed to the surface. An unnatural urge to yank the woman's blonde hair out by the brown roots swept through her. The image of the attendant bald and crying arose in her mind, and it made her flinch at such an unusual surge of crankiness. She was many things, but she wasn't cruel. Alexandria looked at the attendant's name badge.

"Roxanne, I'm in the right seat if this is 11K," Heaving a sigh, Alexandria rubbed the back of her neck with one hand and semi-stood. Sliding over next to the window, she motioned Mr. Hottie into the row area so other passengers could squeeze by.

In the politest voice she could manage, she started over. "I'm sorry. I don't know how it happened, but the airline assigned the same seat to both of us. I have a boarding pass that says 11K, and Mr. ..."

"Ruaidhrí," he supplied.

"Yes, well, Mr. Ruaidhrí seems to have the same seat assignment. Could you please check the computer and get this resolved?" She handed over her boarding pass and for good measure, her Platinum Flight Club Card. Perhaps a little sugar would sweeten the attendant's attitude. "I am a regular in your business class. I know this is unusual and that you'll handle it in short order."

Roxanne seemed less than impressed with Alexandria's platinum status as she eyed the nicely packaged Ruaidhrí. Alexandria got the immediate and distinct impression she was going to get the short end of this stick.

The attendant gave her a cool look and turned to Mr. Ruaidhrí, her demeanor warming considerably. "I'm sorry, but I'll have to speak with operations on this. Miss, please wait here. Mr. Ruaidhrí, you can wait in the first-class cabin, if you like."

He held up his hand. "I'm fine here. We've inconvenienced the other passengers enough. I'll just wait while you work this out."

Dismissed, Roxanne headed down the aisle but glanced back at him with hope in her eyes.

He smiled, as if knowing he would get exactly what he wanted.

Alexandria wanted to puke. "Good grief, do you think everyone does what you want?" she blurted without thinking.

Turning, he shrugged his shoulders. "If they are foolish enough to cater to my whim, they can pay the price." He parked his butt in 11K, put his small pack between his feet, and folded his arms.

She sank a little sideways into the window seat so she could keep him in front of her.

"Fortunately, I don't have the same effect on men. But

yes, most women seem to enjoy doing what I want them to do...or do to them..."

His eyes bored into hers and, as if conjured by his words, an image of him dark, naked, and hard with passion flooded her mind.

Her mouth seemed suddenly dry. As she tried to gather her thoughts, she fidgeted with the phone in her lap. She turned the power off and slipped it into her pocket.

"If it is any consolation," he remarked in good humor, "I'm sure if the attendant had been male, he'd have been panting just as hard to get your attention."

Her jaw dropped. Snapping it shut, she turned purposefully to watch the passengers entering at the front of the cabin.

Tuning out the babble of other passengers settling in for the long flight to Tokyo, Declan observed her as she pointedly ignored him. Frigid winter rain beat on the small window beside her. The cold, bleak weather, in its uniform grayness was at total odds with the fiery woman before him.

Amused by her dismissal, he fought the urge to find out what made her tick. She didn't seem shy. She didn't exhibit the wiles of a practiced flirt. Nor did she jump at the opportunity to "fix" him when he behaved like an ass-hat. He couldn't remember the last woman he'd met who was a true mystery. But then, he didn't get attached to anyone or anything, and he couldn't afford to forget it.

But she *was* lovely, and her disdain was refreshing in a cheeky sort of way.

In profile, her head of riotous red curls resembled blossoms falling in profusion over her shoulder and down to her mid-back. sinfully long, apparently mascara-free lashes fringed radiant emerald-green eyes. But then, her lovely, classic face with high cheekbones and a healthy tanned complexion that spoke of time spent outdoors appeared free of make-up, as well.

Declan was impressed. Most women he'd met wouldn't be caught dead without "putting on their face." He envied her teeth as they tugged on her lower lip. He wished his tongue traced its rim, his teeth nipping at its lushness.

She stretched her long, elegant neck to see if the attendant was coming back. His gaze went to where her pulse beat at her throat. He was sure the smooth skin would taste divine. He wanted to feel the silken touch of her soft curls on his hands. With a slight twinge, he became aware of a growing discomfort in his pants and shook himself for staring at her like a love-struck bull.

A guttural throat-clearing interrupted his thoughts. As one, they both turned their faces toward the noise.

An obese older man stood glaring at her. Sweat beading on his face, he used his left hand to steady himself on the seat in front of Declan while he mopped his brow with a handkerchief. "You're in my seat."

Declan looked at her. They both laughed. Tension rolled away with their laughter. How long had it been since he had just laughed?

Scowling, the irate man waved his boarding pass at them. "Now, see here, miss, this isn't funny. I paid for seat 11L, and I want it right now." The pong of cheap aftershave liberally applied only exacerbated his underlying body odors.

She raised a slender hand to just cover her nose. The movement seemed to add to his irritation. Leaning forward, his heavy paunch pressing against the seat he jabbed a finger in Alexandria's direction. "I think you—"

Declan stood quickly, leaning into the corridor to accommodate his height.

Mr. Sweaty backed up as much as possible in the narrow aisle, craning his neck to stare up at him.

"You'll get your seat, not to worry," Declan said. "It appears the airline issued the same seat to both of us," he gestured to his lovely nemesis, "and they're fixing it right now. We've heard 'You've got my seat' two too many times today and it just struck us funny."

As Declan spoke, the attendant hurried up behind the agitated man. Roxanne squeezed past Mr. Sweaty to place her hand on Declan's forearm.

"Mr. Ruaidhrí, we're so sorry. We don't know how this happened, but 11K was somehow assigned to both of you. To make up for your inconvenience, we will be upgrading you from Business to First Class. If you'll follow me, I'll get you seated."

Declan's peripheral vision caught the look of dismay on her face at the same moment he saw understanding sink into Mr. Sweaty. His satisfied leer raised Declan's hackles.

The thought of this obnoxious bastard sitting next to the stunning young woman irritated him beyond reason. Before years of habit could intervene, his long-suppressed chivalry took a leap of faith.

Declan reached out and took the attendant's hand in his, looking into her eyes to be sure he had her attention, while Mr. Sweaty huffed to ensure his annoyance was noted.

"Listen," Declan turned to look at her and raised his brows in question.

"Alexandria," she supplied.

"Alexandria and I are already here and poor Mr...?" he inquired to Mr. Sweaty.

"Johnson, the name's Johnson," he wheezed.

"Yes, Mr. Johnson here is the one who has truly been inconvenienced, waiting in the aisle and dealing with our confusion. Please give him the upgrade and we'll call it even, no harm done."

Although Roxanne and Johnson stared wide-eyed at him, he focused on Alexandria's surprised gasp. He swept the attendant around to face Johnson.

Roxanne seemed about to protest but relented in the face of Johnson's growing excitement at his good fortune. "Certainly, Mr. Ruaidhrí, if that is your wish. Mr. Johnson, if you will follow me this way." She squeezed past Johnson and led the way to the forward cabin.

Declan settled back into his seat and turned to face Alexandria.

On one hand, she looked relieved not to have to sit next to the sweaty jerk, but she definitely didn't look pleased that he would be her seat partner.

"Declan," he said, holding out his hand. "Declan Ruaidhrí."

"Ruaidhrí? Wasn't that the given name of the last high king of Ireland?" Alexandria shook his hand.

An electric jolt shot right down his spine and into his dick. "Ahem, yes." He cleared his throat. "But when my great-grandfather, who was named for him, immigrated, they inverted his names and he became Conall Ruaidhrí'. And the rest, as they say, is history." He shrugged; the girl was no one's fool. He adjusted in his seat. "Seems they did a lot of name changing back in the day."

"Have you lived there?" Her cheeks pinkened as if the inquiry were too personal. "I couldn't place your accent."

"Among other places, yes. We 'migrated' a lot when I was a kid, and my accent picked up a little bit of everywhere. It was all part and parcel of my dad's work. Alexandria is pretty unusual." He grinned. "Are your parents Egyptologists or librarians?"

She laughed.

The sound kicked his pulse up a notch--or twenty.

"No. Mother loved the unusual and had a mind to name us for her favorite places." She pointed to the floorspace in front of him. "If you'll hand me the case under the seat in front of you, you'll have more leg room."

Declan pulled out the case and passed it to her. She slipped her iPad from the side pocket and put it in the seat-back pocket, tipping the case to angle it under the seat in front of her.

The name placard said 'A. Marsh' and he offhandedly said, "No relation to Edin Marsh, by chance?"

She almost dropped the case. "Yes, he's my brother."

"No shit!" The expletive escaped before he could control himself. Just as fast, the realization that he could not seduce this woman drove itself home. Somehow, "Shit, oh shit, and no shit" seemed grossly inadequate. *Fuck! This is Edin's mysterious sister that he never talks about?* What were the issues between them? She sure as hell didn't look like Edin or John. Those two looked so alike, with their glacier-blue eyes and blue-black hair. They appeared cold and distant until you got to know them. He would have expected a strong family resemblance in a sister. Alexandria was fire to their ice. Red hair, green eyes, passion thrumming under the surface of her skin, beckoning him like a siren's call. Was she adopted?

Wide-eyed, she looked at him like he'd grown horns.

"Sorry about that, Edin's my attorney. I didn't mean any offense."

"No, that wasn't it. I was just so startled. What are the odds?" Her voice trailed off as she turned to look out the window.

Declan felt her pull back from him mentally, like she had stepped inside a fence and was closing the gate in his face. "Hey, you okay?"

"Yes," she murmured, almost to herself.

As he watched her worry her fingers, staring out into the storm, Declan wondered for a moment if she was mental. Perhaps that was why Edin didn't talk about her. Just the mention of the family tie seemed to set loose a maelstrom of tension and anxiety.

Although tumultuous thoughts catapulted through Alexandria's mind, she displayed the nonchalance of a seasoned traveler, giving minimal attention to the flight attendants who were securing the cabin for take-off. As she fastened her seat belt and removed the airline blanket and pillow from their plastic bags, her thoughts whirled.

Declan pulled his iPad out of his pack, put it in his seat-back pocket, and slid the pack under the seat. His broad shoulders filled the seat, touching hers.

As they taxied toward the runway the attendants started in on the mandatory safety procedures. Alexandria fought to focus on the words. Anything to distract from Declan. In such tight quarters, she couldn't ignore his scent, warm and earthy, or the heat that seemed to touch her in all the wrong places.

Is he on his way to see Edin? Is this just a freaky coinci-

dence? If he's going to see him, is Edin up to some weird matchmaking scheme? Was this why he and Dad forced my promise, knowing I would never break my word.

"So, are you on your way to Isola delle Lacrime?" As she searched his face, waiting for his answer, panic gripped her.

"Are you?" he countered, his tone unexpectedly gentle.

"Yes, Edin and Dad made me promise to come for the holidays."

Alexandria could see he was baffled, as well as intrigued, by her anxiety, so she tried to turn his thoughts in a safer direction. She couldn't very well have him going where she feared to tread.

"I absolutely love Christmas and am happiest to celebrate it in a Norman Rockwell winter wonderland setting," she babbled. "Snow, icicles, the local church Nativity scene, cookies and homemade goodies, trees, wreaths, decorations..." Her list, like her voice, started to trail off.

The curve of his smile lit his eyes, making them more blue than gray.

If she'd thought he was gorgeous before, he was dazzling now.

"It just doesn't seem like Christmas on a tropical island, sweat running down your back and sand in your shorts."

"Exactly." She laughed and the warmth of it soothed away much of her tension. And perhaps, if she was honest with herself, the attention of a handsome man was nice. She hadn't allowed herself the luxury of finding any man alluring in so long.

"I know. It's not my idea of Christmas, either. But yes, I'm also on my way there. Edin extracted a promise from me, as well. The last couple of years have been tough, and a little R&R was in order."

Shadows crossed Declan's face. Alexandria wondered

what had been tough but wasn't sure she wanted to know, afraid either compassion or kinship might bloom.

"Anyway..." Declan rubbed the back of his neck with his hand. "Edin's a good guy, and he convinced me to come for the holidays. He promised a great vacation, really peaceful, where I'd have plenty of privacy and quiet time to recharge the batteries."

Alexandria felt a guilty twinge. Her brother loved her and wouldn't play matchmaker behind her back. She should not have doubted him. Apparently, the man before her had redeeming qualities that Edin recognized, and Edin had offered him a much-needed retreat. The least she could do was be civil. If only he didn't exude an electric sexual energy that made the very air around her feel charged. This was going to be the longest flight of her life. Well, maybe not the longest, but definitely the most uncomfortable.

Her left hand lay in her lap and the fingers of her right hand absently stroked the back of it. "The island is beautiful. If you're looking for peace and quiet, it's the perfect place. Because of Dad's business, he maintains several private bungalows on the property for guests, as well as rooms in the house. Some people prefer more privacy than others."

"Edin said as much." Declan joined her in the haze of polite but distant conversation.

Casually, as if the answer didn't matter, she asked, "Do you know if Edin invited anyone else?"

Declan's eyebrows arched, and he tilted his head to regard her. "Actually, I'm under the impression that I'm the only non-family member invited, other than Meredith. She's nice and, if I remember correctly, doesn't have any family."

A pang of regret and a stab of resentment swept through

her that a complete stranger knew more of what was happening in her family than she did. *If Brent wasn't such a petty little bastard, I wouldn't be so alienated from my brother.* She wasn't even familiar with Edin's girlfriend. Alexandria knew her name but had yet to meet the woman who had held her brother's fancy longer than anyone in the past. She stared out the window and watched the landscape fly by during the thrust of take-off and then fade into a distant blur as they reached cruising altitude.

She might as well confirm if this was going to be the most uncomfortable trip she'd ever been on. "So, flight 881 to Tokyo, United 197 to Tamuning, and United 174 to Saipan?"

He nodded.

Nearly thirty hours of travel time and two plane changes loomed on the horizon. After which, the little matter of an hour boat ride would land lock her for two weeks with the sexiest male she had ever seen. *No sweat, right?* Hopefully, they would be seated at opposite ends of the next two planes.

Her mother had drilled manners into her children, and Alexandria knew she would have to find a polite way to interact with Declan for the next two weeks. Perhaps, if she got to know him a little better, the effects she was feeling from his presence would dissipate. "Have you met Dad and Margaret?"

"Your dad, yes, but I haven't had the chance to meet Margaret yet."

"You'll love her. My stepmother is a fabulous hostess and has a wicked sense of humor. She's been really good for my dad."

"So, I take it your perception of her is not the stereotypical evil stepmother," he teased.

20

"No. I've known Margaret all my life. She and her husband, James, were my parents' best friends. Edin and my god parents, too." Her teeth tugged at her lip. "My mother was the most amazing woman on earth. The way she and my dad loved each other...well, let's just say that as a kid, I used to get embarrassed by them. But as I got older, I felt lucky to see such a love. It's rare. I know he loved my mother truly and deeply. She knew it, and she would've wanted him to be happy again."

He opened his mouth, hesitated, and shut it.

"What?" Alexandria asked.

Declan flushed. "Your dad married your god mother? Wasn't that weird for you?"

At his obvious discomfort, Alexandria nearly laughed, but something in his eyes held her back. A soft gentle smile bought her time to measure her words. "My parents and god parents were two of the happiest, most loving couples I've ever seen. Each of them knew they had married their 'soul mates', for lack of a better terminology."

"You don't believe in soul mates?" Declan asked.

"No, I don't." Alexandria shifted in her seat.

Declan tapped his heart with his hand. "Wow, I think that's the first time I've ever heard a woman say that. Since the day I hit puberty, it seems like every girl I've met has been telling me that we're soul mates."

Alexandria laughed at his playfulness. "Oh, really? I find that hard to believe. Were you the only boy in town?" As he grinned, she laughed again.

"Well, as a matter of fact, sometimes, yes." He laughed with her.

Alexandria sobered after a moment. She fiddled with the end of her seatbelt. "Regardless, soul mate theory aside, when my dad told me he and Margaret were getting married, it just seemed right. They each had the love of their lives and knew how to love another. I read somewhere that people who have truly loved are more likely to remarry happily. I'm thrilled my dad is blessed with two happy marriages."

I wonder if I'll ever even have one.

CHAPTER TWO

As the jet taxied away from the gate, an older man in a dark gray overcoat moved closer to the windows. "Yes, I'm sure," he rasped into the cell phone. "I've been tailing marks all my life and I saw yours board flight 881 to Tokyo."

"You saw this? How did you get past security?" the cold voice questioned.

"I'm fuckin' good at what I do, and I got connections." He ran his hand through his graying hair. Man, this client was a tool. "You're paying good money for this info. Do you want it or not?"

"Yes. And if you don't learn a little respect, this could be the last mark you ever tail."

He swallowed the lump in his throat. He just wanted to get paid and get clear of this deal before shit went south. "My source tells me the final flight destination is Saipan, but from there...."

"I don't need an itinerary. I paid you to verify departure and destination. I know exactly what happens from there."

The line went quiet, so he looked at the screen to

confirm the call was ended. He thrust the phone in his coat pocket. *I gotta get a new job. These crazy fucking stalkers are bat shit nuts. Someday, one of them might just come after me.*

CHAPTER THREE

Declan watched Alexandria glance a little sadly out the window and wondered if her thoughts were in the past with her mother or unsure of something in her present. He cleared the lump in his throat. "I used to question if my parents even liked each other, the way they would bicker and argue, but then I figured out that they wouldn't have it any other way. God help the sorry soul who tried to get between them."

"Like a tennis match?"

Puzzled, it took him a second to react. "Excuse me?"

She waved her hands side-to-side. "The banter...like a tennis match, back and forth, back and forth. Mom and Dad used to give me whiplash trying to follow some of their debates."

He nodded. "I wouldn't call my parents' matches something as civilized as debates."

She laughed.

Glad to have chased away her sadness, Declan diverted the conversation to safer ground. Although he wasn't sure any such thing as safer ground existed with such an intriguing creature.

His conversational skills hadn't been worked this hard since...well, ever. Books, movies, world events, topic after topic flew by.

She hid a yawn.

"I should let you get some rest," he said. "Perhaps we both should."

"That's probably a good idea." Alexandria reclined her seat and shook out her travel blanket. "I didn't get much sleep last night."

"Saying holiday goodbyes to the boyfriend?" The mental kick in his ass was hard. As Alexandria raised her brows, Declan put his hands up in mock surrender. "Sorry. I shouldn't have said that. It's none of my business."

"Thanks for figuring that out on your own." She fluffed her travel pillow. "And no--there's no one to say goodbye to." She turned toward the window and snuggled into her pillow.

An odd sense of relief washed over him. For a moment, Declan watched her before he, too, reclined his seat. But his restless mind would not settle, and his perusal kept straying to the still form beside him.

His reaction to her puzzled him. Why did she intrigue him so? She was gorgeous, he'd left a long line of beautiful women in his wake. But then, his focus with women wasn't usually conversation. That had to be it. The conversation. Her easy rapport had made him want to discuss his life and business--topics he never discussed. But more than that, she had also diverted any conversation of a personal nature to neutral topics. Usually, he felt like he was being interrogated at worst or, at best, in a job interview. The lack of pressure had been relaxing. He just wasn't used to having a conversation without measuring every word.

As he forced himself to close his eyes, he heard a little voice say, *Right.*

———

Declan was a mystery to Alexandria. After the disclosure of her relationship to Edin, he had dropped the sexual innuendoes. Companionable small talk about irrelevant things that ate up the hours.

Despite her protests, he escorted her courteously from one flight to the next in Tokyo, citing he was sure Edin would not approve of him leaving her to fend for herself in a foreign country. She had almost laughed in his face, but seeing his serious expression, she held back.

On the flight to Tamuning, he seemed more than a little put out to find himself sitting on the opposite aisle, one row back from her. Alexandria tried not to show her relief at putting a little distance between them. She *was* tired, and the hour or so she had tried to sleep on the last flight had added more to her agitated state than relieved it. Despite her efforts to still her wayward mind, she had lain awake, vacillating between thoughts of the very intriguing Declan and how she could keep her secrets from her family.

Her row companion for the Tamuning flight had been a chatty college age male on his way to the Naval Base at Guam to meet his father for the holidays. He'd attempted to hit on her from the start. He wasn't getting the hints she was dropping and when he went to the lavatory, Declan slid into the young man's seat. When the youthful Casanova returned, Declan handed the youth his small carryon and point-blank directed him to the seat Declan had vacated.

He opened his mouth to protest, but a hard look from Declan changed his mind. Jaw clamped shut, he slunk to the empty seat like a pouty child. Declan smiled, reclined his seat and took a nap.

She dozed, as well. As she awoke, she peeked from under her lashes to find him watching her with hungry eyes. He averted his gaze and slipped back into the role of polite acquaintance.

In Tamuning, he'd left nothing to chance and she'd watched him accost the first United ticket counter agent he could grab to ensure side-by-side seats. His determined efforts to chaperone her were kinda cute. Unnecessary, but cute.

As the Boeing 737-800 rolled to a stop on the tarmac at Saipan International Airport, Declan turned to her. "Well, you ready for this?"

Like a bucket of ice water, his simple question took her breath away and she stared at him, mouth slightly ajar.

He gave her an odd look. "It's probably in the high eighties outside. It was barely thirty when we left Chicago."

"Oh," Alexandria mumbled. She gave him the shadow of a smile. "I'm as ready as I'll ever be."

God help me if I'm not.

Alexandria's heart clenched at the sight of Edin texting, leaning against the handrail. Her beautiful brother. He looked up, and she stopped in her tracks.

Declan paused with the luggage cart, glancing from one to the other.

Edin pushed off the handrail, shoved the phone into his pocket, and bounded toward her.

She dashed forward and jumped into his arms. Being swept up in his arms and held close was like cool water after a long hot drought. Kisses peppered her face, and she laughed, a deep, joyful laugh, for the first time in what felt like forever. Happy tears bubbled over and Edin brushed them away. "I'm glad to see you too, baby sis."

She smiled but couldn't speak. She saw the sheen of tears in his eyes and blinked to clear her own.

Hugging him close, she turned with him to face Declan, who watched with a puzzled smile, as if a clue to a mystery had gone awry.

A final quick kiss to her forehead, and Edin left her arms to greet Declan, clasping him in a macho hug, complete with the ritualistic male back pounding.

As she watched their greeting, Alexandria's teeth tugged at her lip. Declan meant something to Edin. Her brother didn't hug other men.

"Good to see you, man," Edin said.

"Likewise," Declan replied.

Edin glanced between them. "Well, I see you two saved me the trouble of introducing you. How did you manage that?"

"You won't believe us." As Declan pushed the luggage cart forward, he clapped Edin on the shoulder. Edin and Alexandria fell in beside him. "It was hard not to meet since we were assigned the same seat out of Chicago."

"The same seat..." Edin's voice trailed off.

Alexandria looped her arm through her brother's and smiled across him at Declan. "Yeah, wait 'til you hear this story."

CHAPTER FOUR

Azure skies stretched from one horizon to the other. The blue-and-white thirty-five-foot Monterey super sport Bowrider sliced through the swells of the Pacific Ocean, chasing the sun as it headed west. Warm rays from the golden early afternoon sun beat down on the craft as it skimmed its course over the blue-green vastness.

Leaning back in the seat, sea spray hit Alexandria in the face. She swept out her arm, trying to catch water in her hand while the boat sped toward Isola delle Lacrime. In the distance, she could see the teardrop-shaped island, named for its outline, rising from the crystalline blue waters around it. At the pointed end of the tear, high, rocky bluffs faced eastward. Waves crashed on jagged boulders and slabs of cliff face that had sheared off and collapsed over time, forming a protective stone barrier that absorbed the bulk of the Pacific Ocean's battering surf.

Formed long ago by the volcanic activity in the area, the high point of the island tapered off to the long white sandy beaches which formed the rounded bottom of the tear. Tropical jungle terrain cascaded from the peak down to the beaches. A quarter mile from shore, a reef acted as a natural breakwater, circling three quarters of the island and protecting the shorelines from the strong ocean surge.

The fact that her dad OWNED an island still boggled her mind. Mind you, it was a small one, but still, he *owned* a whole island. She swelled with pride at her father's accomplishments. They had never been poor, but her dad was tenacious in the drive to build his shipping empire, always emphasizing to his children that the road to success was paved with hard work and appreciation. The acquisition of the island when she was in middle school had been a benchmark of his achievements.

Mid-way up from the beach to the bluffs, a large flattened area bisected the landmass where the main house presided over the lower western coastline. At the crystal-clear lagoon, a handful of over-the-water bungalows connected to the main beach area by wooden docks. Located far enough from shore but close enough to the reef line, swimmers found it easy to snorkel or sit on the docks and watch the jewel-toned fish cavort.

Her attention turned to her brother. Six-foot-two, just like Dad, Edin looked like a younger version of her father. Apparently, he had been putting in his sun time since his arrival. The golden tan he sported set off his white board shorts.

By Edin's side, larger than life, Declan stood, taking in the island.

He was a mystery to her. After the disclosure of her relationship to Edin, he had dropped the flirtatious behaviors. Well, mostly. The three flights had actually passed in companionable politeness, except for the sensual charge he exuded.

Edin throttled back, and the Bowrider sank into a

relaxed forward glide through the swells as they neared the reef line.

Alexandria came to her feet and moved to half kneel on the seat behind Edin. As she propped her chin on his shoulder, he turned his head to smile at her.

Turning back to the helm, Edin swept his hand from right to left. "Well, here she is, Isola delle Lacrime—commonly known to us gringos as Island of Tears."

Declan shot Edin a dry look. "Um, isn't Isola delle Lacrime an Italian name?"

"Well, yes. Mom gave it the Italian version when Dad acquired the title. Before that, it carried the Spanish name Isla de las Lágrimas, which dated back to the original European explorations when many of the native islanders and their cultures were killed off. The natives believed because the island was shaped like a tear drop that it was a holding place for all the tears shed by their people. She wanted to preserve its history but not its sadness."

Alexandria perked up. "I remember that. From the moment she saw it Mom was adamant the island would only be a place for happy tears."

Edin pointed to the lagoon where the six thatched bungalows spread out like pearls on a necklace of wooden walkways. "These are the over-water bungalows we talked about. They are pretty basic. Each has a self-contained bathroom. Kinda like an RV, but the difference is our staff can pull the tanks and store them in heavy weather. The storms here can be fierce and we don't want any brown water polluting the lagoon."

Declan smiled. "Very green of you."

Edin shrugged. "We try. They don't have any kitchens, though, just mini fridges. All the food is served at the main house." He pointed with both hands, palms up, across the lagoon to the wide sandy beach and beyond. "And there she is."

Declan's gaze rose to take in the house set into the hillside about halfway up the long slope of the island. Declan whistled.

The low, appreciative sound danced up Alexandria's spine. Easing back from Edin to stand in between the rear seats, she raised a hand to shield the glare from the water and pretended to study the house. A large main section sat dead center at the widest point of the bluff with two wings extending off in each direction. As he described the house like old friend, tension coiled, squeezing her heart.

"When Dad originally got the island, the house, if you could call it that, was down by the harbor. Mom designed this one."

Alexandria was glad for the sunglasses that hid the tears welling in her eyes. With a discreet swipe of her finger she swept the moisture away.

Edin pointed at the main center structure. "The main compound is round like a giant disk. It takes up most of the open flat space. The kitchen, pantry, theater room and a couple of restrooms lie along the back side. The dining area is dead center and everything on this side is one large open great room where people can gather."

"Looks interesting. How would you describe that style? It kinda looks like Mid-Century Modern and Mediterranean hooked up."

Edin laughed at Declan's description. "Sort of. Mom wanted the warmth and hospitality of Mediterranean design but the function of something more modern. This entire side has full-height glass doors that rotate on a center axis and slide back on a track system, so the great room and deck combine for bigger social settings."

"Wow. I didn't know your Mom was an architect."

"She wasn't, but she could have been. I think she drove a few good men to new heights with her demands. You'll find most of the wood furniture and cabinetry was milled from either fallen timber on the island or trees excavated for the construction. Mom wanted to recycle every single thing she took out. " Edin pointed toward the right wing. "That is the family wing." His hand swung to indicate the left wing. "And on that side, is the guest wing. You'll have rooms on that side."

"Rooms?" Declan asked. "I thought I was in a bungalow with a well-stocked mini-fridge." He smiled at his pal.

Edin coughed. "The mini-fridge in your room is stocked, I'm sure. But you're not in a bungalow. You're in the guest wing. Margaret's orders. Most rooms have a least a bedroom, a sitting area,and a private bathroom."

Declan raised his brows.

At the thought of Declan in the main house, languid warmth coiled in Alexandria's belly. Pushing it away, she turned her focus from their banter to truly examine the home her mother had built. Set into the hillside, the house blended into the jungle around it. Like an old friend, it sat with a patient smile--waiting for her to renew her acquaintance. The beautiful, ivory, Mediterranean stucco skeleton carried the open, modern window elements with grace.

Edin throttled up, and the Bowrider surged forward. Alexandria curled into the seat while he skillfully maneuvered the boat toward the channel in the reef which would give them access to the protected harbor. On the southeastern side of the island, a small, but deep, inlet cut inland providing a suitable harbor area for the boats during all but the most severe of Mother Nature's tempests. Two sturdy docks serviced most of the island traffic, and four offshore moorings handled any overflow.

Alexandria's face turned to the family wing of the house. Dark wood framed windows ran floor to ceiling from the wing's connection at the great room until the final curve which tucked back into the hillside. Unlike the full-height glass of the great room, the wide, short bottom windows were stationary while the top two thirds were a series of panels that slid on three tracks, allowing the occupant to push them aside to welcome the slightest zephyr to their side. When open, the sheer ivory curtain panels would billow in the breeze.

She hadn't wanted any curtains to detract from her view. That was one argument she had lost. Her mother had insisted on "sheers for a modicum of privacy" and the roll down shades which could darken the suite on the brightest of days. She still hadn't used those.

As she pictured her rooms, or more accurately--her room, her throat tightened. Countless hours spent with Mom during the design process, reviewing every detail. Mom had wanted separate rooms for sitting, sleeping, and closets, but Alexandria had wanted one big room without division. In the end, she'd gotten her way on that. Her one concession was the small toilet enclosure, which hadn't been so much concession as good taste, but she had still debated it with Mom just for the fun of it. Her double suite doors opened to a wide vista. The jungle dropped away on the steep hillside below the softly curving window line which provided a nearly one-hundred-eighty-degree view of the sea.

To the right of the entry doors, on the wall from the windows to the corridor, low cabinets with a Spanish gold marble counter provided storage, as well as a happy home to the mini-fridge and a wet bar area. Above the counter, carved wooden masks hung on either side of a framed copy of Rousseau's *Tiger in a Tropical Storm*.

At the corner, the lower cabinets turned along the interior wall and became a deep built-in desk with drawers and storage. Atop the counter, ceiling height built-in bookshelves ran from the corner to the doors. Framed photos, books, and countless memorabilia littered the shelves.

To the left of the suite doors, wooden, floor-to-ceiling cabinets functioned as closets, shoe storage, and built-in dressers. A wry smile turned Alexandria's lips as she thought of how empty the twenty feet of storage was. She had never taken to shopping the way her mother had hoped.

The closet wall ended at the back of the toilet enclosure where a low wall jutted out which separated the marble counter and sink of the restroom area from the rest of the space. Across from the bathroom counter, a large spa-style bathtub nestled against the outer window wall allowing a bather to enjoy a hot soak while admiring the sunset. Next to the tub and across from the toilet, a large glass-and-marble shower occupied the corner.

Hues of tan and ivory dominated the décor with accents in varying shades of coral and a beautiful blue that anchored the ocean vista beyond the window line. A king-sized, four-poster bed, draped with mosquito netting, sat in the open area in front of the closet space. A side table by the bed, and a bench by the closet, delineated the sleeping portion of the room, while two chairs, a couple of accent tables, and a large, sapphire blue, two-person chaise by the windows graced the other half of the room.

She had spent countless hours on the chaise, sometimes with a good book or cuddled with Mom looking at magazines. Smiling in remembrance of how her mother's exasperation with the "one big room" concept had turned to praise at the end result, she turned her attention back to Edin.

As the Bowrider glided closer to the quay, a lump grew in her throat at the sight of her father walking toward the mooring area. Her eyes threatened to leak again, and she blinked rapidly to clear them. She smiled and waved as Edin maneuvered the boat closer to the wharf. Declan moved to the lines at the forward bow, and she took the stern line. They threw the lines to the waiting dock hands for tie up and went to gather their possessions.

Declan's hand brushed hers as he snagged her camera case, and the now- familiar surge of excitement shot through her.

"Why don't you hop on the dock," he said, "and I'll hand everything over?"

"Works for me." She leapt to the dock and reached back for the case. Before she could take it, Edin was there, claiming the case from Declan.

"Go see Dad, we'll handle this. I'll take good care of your life's blood." Edin gave the case a gentle shake.

With a quick smile, she turned and sprinted the short distance to her dad. As with Edin, he swept her into a tight embrace and whirled her around in circles.

Declan watched her go and turned to Edin. "Life's blood?"

"Didn't she tell you? She's a photographer, a damn fine one too. World class. *National Geographic, The Smithsonian, Conde Nast, Travel & Leisure*, all the big guns want her."

Confusion and comprehension tangled in Declan's mind. Stock still, he stared at Edin.

"SHE is Al Marsh?"

"Yeah," Edin said as he continued to heft the other supplies from the boat to the dock. After a moment, he stopped to look at Declan. "Why?

Scowling, Declan turned to Edin. "I guess I'll ask her myself why she turned down the contract to shoot the Kukenam Tepui expedition. Hank said Marsh wasn't interested in the least, and the fee quoted verged on extortion."

Edin paused his unloading efforts. "Hank tried to hire her?"

Declan thrust a box into Edin's hands. "Yeah. Shouldn't you know that? You are my attorney."

Shrugging, Edin put the box on the dock. "I've been tied up with licensing your new drug lines and finalizing your FDA approvals. Associates have been handling most of your routine stuff the last couple of months."

"Well, maybe you could work your brotherly magic and put in a good word. Hank said he got shut down so fast he never got out of the gate."

Edin smiled. "Sorry, pal, but that doesn't sound like our Al. Inaccessible jungle, tough terrain, critters aplenty— that's her kind of party. She always accepts the tough stuff over the fluff."

Irritation that he hadn't put two and two together before now warred with a surge of respect in Declan. He was familiar with some of the "tough stuff" Al Marsh had shot. He'd seen the photos in museums. Their poignant beauty had stirred him to have his expedition coordinator find and hire Al, regardless of the cost. To be denied that talent irked him. He wasn't used to being denied.

The golden, tropical light of a waning, late afternoon sun soaked Alexandria's room. Being the last suite on the family wing had its advantages. It was quiet. Plus, the full-height wall of windows that faced the setting sun curved enough on the south side to give her an unobstructed view of the southern sky.

Naked, Alexandria rolled from her stomach to her back and flung her arms wide on the king- size bed, stretching like a big, happy cat. Eyes closed, she luxuriated in the feel of the silken breeze from the open windows sliding across her skin. A vision of Declan similarly nuzzling her was accompanied by an electric tingle racing over her and a flood of molten heat into her core. She sat upright in a rush, staring about the room as if he were going to pop out from behind the sheer curtains.

Her eyes landed on the bedside clock. *Shit. Five-thirty.* She was due poolside at six o'clock. Naptime was definitely over. Crossing the international date line and losing a day was always tough. Her body knew she had left mid-day Saturday, her mind knew it was Monday evening and Christmas Eve to boot, but the thirty hours of travel time and jet lag still made her feel like it was Sunday night and time to fall into bed.

Knowing she couldn't nap forever or avoid the family for long, Alexandria rolled out of bed and headed for the shower. No sense in prolonging the inevitable—fruity drinks, appetizers, avoid any detailed conversations. No problem. *Right.*

An elbow on the bar, Declan rolled the neck of the cold Hefeweizen between his thumb and forefinger.

"Distracted much?"

Edin's voice snapped him out of his reverie. He looked straight at Edin but the view in his peripheral vision momentarily short-circuited his smart-ass reply. "Apparently so. Maybe you should have told me your sister made you look like the ass end of an ugly bull."

Edin laughed. "If I had told you that, you wouldn't have come. Skip the shit where I wouldn't try to match-make anybody for love or money." Making a gagging face, he shook himself.

Declan glanced from Edin to Alexandria. Across the pool she stood at the railing, chatting and watching the sunset with Margaret. Khaki cargo shorts accentuated her long, toned legs. His palms itched, jealous of the body-hugging tan tank top curving around her breasts.

She was smiling and laughing with Margaret. The sound of her laughter rolled across the pool and over him; the joy of it disturbed him. His stomach tightened and his hands started to sweat. He stared at her, willing her to stop laughing.

"Declan."

Edin's voice was serious, and Declan turned his face to look him square in the eye.

"Declan. I..." Edin's focus seemed to waiver.

"Just spit it out, E. What's on your mind?"

"Listen, I might be your attorney and I definitely have my two cents to put in on every deal, every expedition, every business transaction you make." Edin tilted his head in Alex's general direction. "But I'm telling you now, not as your attorney, but as your friend, leave her alone."

"Edin, you know me better than most. I don't get involved with the kind of woman a man keeps and you know it. I screw 'em and kiss 'em goodbye. If for no other reason than she is your sister, she'd be safe with me."

Edin's gaze dropped a bit and he half smiled. "I know, I'm sorry."

Declan couldn't resist screwing with him. "But, for argument's sake, what if she doesn't want me to leave her alone?"

Edin snorted. "She doesn't know what she wants. She works over ninety percent of the year in remote shithole locations, taking photos of God knows what. Every year for the last four years, she has come home at Christmas and holed up in the house our grandmother left her in Manitowoc. She doesn't date. She doesn't socialize. She doesn't go out. Nothing."

"Why?"

Edin looked down at the beer in his hands and swirled the bottle.

"Our mom died of cancer in the summer of that year. She loved Christmas. Mom and Al used to drive Dad and me nuts with the baking, decorating, shopping and all that other girly holiday crap. But it was their favorite time of year, and we were always together for it. No matter what Al was working on, she made sure she was there for the season."

Declan's throat tightened. He watched Edin swallow hard and pause to focus his thoughts.

"When I was a kid, it drove me crazy that Al was forever doggin' my heels. But somewhere along the way, she became my best friend, not just my sister. We used to do pretty much everything together. She was in college when I started with the firm, we hung with the same people. She was engaged to one of my law partners."

The thought of Alexandria being engaged irritated the

shit out of Declan, but the thought of her in pain made his stomach churn.

"What happened?"

"Mom died and to some extent, Dad and I think Al did too. She took it really hard, and a short time later, she withdrew from everyone we knew. She stormed into my office one morning when Brent and I were reviewing a case, broke off their engagement, and walked out before I could really get a handle on what had happened. I've hardly seen her in the last four years."

"What do you mean, you've hardly seen her? She's your damn sister. Why the hell not?"

The indignant, possessive tone didn't go unnoticed. Edin's eyes went cold, and Declan knew he had overstepped. "I just mean that if she was my sister, I wouldn't have let her shut me out like that."

"Since that day in my office Al travels most of the time-- from January to November at minimum. Typically, she only comes home for any length of time for December. If she stops in during the year, it's unannounced and she's an expert at getting in and out unnoticed. She ditched her apartment in Chicago and moved everything to the house in Manitowoc. At one hundred and seventy miles from Chicago, she effectively isolated her home from drop-in visitors. The first couple of years, Dad and I respected her need to have time to grieve. But afterwards...I don't know, we couldn't reach her, and we didn't know what to do. I think we thought time heals all."

"So, what happened that she's back in the family bosom now?"

A wry smile flitted over Edin's face and was gone. "Call it an intervention if you like, but we double-teamed her."

Declan choked on his beer. "You what?"

"We had the neighbor call us when she got home, and we showed up on her doorstep. Told her we weren't taking no for an answer, and that she had to come spend Christmas with us."

"Four years and she capitulated just like that?"

"Well, no. That's the short-short version. We were there for hours trying to cram the idea down her throat, but she didn't agree until we told her we'd be on Isola delle Lacrime. Seemed funny, but I thought maybe it was easier for her if we weren't there where we all celebrated with Mom. We're just worried about what happens when she goes home. She's got to get out of the past and into the present."

A newfound esteem for the Marsh family augmented Declan's comments. "Edin, everyone has their story," Declan said, watching Alexandria across the pool. "Anyone who says they don't have any baggage is just hiding it in a storage container. She's strong and intelligent; she'll find her way, especially with your love and support." He looked back at Edin and didn't care for the speculative gleam in his friend's eyes.

"So...buddy...you're telling me you have a supercargo somewhere full of your shit?"

Declan smiled. "You kiddin'?" he said. "I sank that mother."

CHAPTER FIVE

The violets and purples of a waning sunset painted the cloud-littered horizon, while the soft light of twilight ebbed before the glow of warm golden mini-lights strung over the pool deck.

Margaret had stood quietly beside her as the sun sank into the Pacific, watching for a flash of green. A tightening of her throat reminded Alexandria of the times she waited for the rare phenomena, sandwiched between her mother and her godmother.

Margaret looked good. The last time Alexandria had seen her she had been in mourning. First for her husband, James, who had died eleven and half months before Alexandria's mother, and then for both her husband and best friend. She'd been pale and stressed then. But now she glowed. Happiness agreed with her and she wore her beauty well. She had always reminded Alexandria of Ilsa Lund in the iconic *Casablanca*.

Alexandria laughed at Margaret's recounting of her first spear-fishing experience. She maneuvered to a position where she could look at Margaret or over her shoulder at

Edin and Declan lounging against the bar area on the far side of the pool.

They seemed deep in discussion and she wondered what had Edin looking so serious. Perhaps the invitation to Declan had a business motive.

Declan turned his head to watch her. The angry glare in his eyes took her off-guard. Surely, that was not meant for her. She lost track of Margaret's last comment and had to ask her to repeat it. Margaret glanced from her to the bar, and with a warm smile, hooked Alexandria's arm with hers.

"Enough of me. Let's go see what those handsome devils at the bar are up to."

In short order, Alexandria found herself being towed around the pool. With every step closer to the bar, her heartbeat picked up speed until she felt the rush of blood coursing through her veins, dragging excitement along for the ride. This was ridiculous! It was her brother and his friend.

"I don't know what's going on over here, but you two look way too deep in thought for my taste on Christmas Eve."

Both men smiled at Margaret, but Edin was quick on the uptake.

"Sorry, Margaret, it's all Declan's fault. He won't shut the hell up about business."

At the stunned look on Declan's face, Alexandria almost burst out laughing. He recovered quickly and shot a glance at Alexandria before focusing on Margaret.

"Sorry. Edin is a boring conversationalist so I had to resort to business." The wicked grin on his face belied the sting of the words, and they all laughed.

"Well, you can just talk to Al. She has fantastic conversation skills." Margaret laid down the law. "And I won't hear any more about business for the day."

Shocked, Alexandria was unable to speak for a moment.

"Since Edin has such serious shortcomings," Declan grasped the opportunity, "Perhaps Alexandria could give me the grand tour?"

"I think you should stick with Edin," she shot back. The chilling glance Edin gave Declan reminiscent of her younger days, when Edin had chased away anyone he thought unworthy of her. She wasn't up to that drama right now. "I haven't been here in a long time."

Margaret turned from Alexandria to Declan. "Well, we'll leave the tour guide debate for a dinner topic. I'm sure John and Meredith are waiting for us in the dining room by now."

Margaret put her hand on Edin's arm, forcing him to escort her. "Declan, why don't you escort Alexandria to Christmas Eve dinner?"

Declan almost laughed at Alexandria's wide-eyed look as she watched Edin lead Margaret toward the house. It seemed silly to formally escort anyone in hot, humid weather, wearing shorts and flip flops, but what the hell? With affected gallantry, he held out his arm to her. She looked about to bolt before she relented, a smile tugging at her lush mouth, and allowed him to tuck her arm in his.

Declan felt the current of her touch in the way the fine hairs of his arms came to attention. For that matter, something else was coming to attention in her proximity, and he better find a way to fix that. He wanted no quarrel with

Edin or John over her. As it was, he had no idea what possessed him to propose her as his tour guide.

Walking toward the house, he sensed anxiety in her, as well. At the threshold of the great room where large glass panels folded back to open the interior to the pool deck, he watched her turn inward, uncertainty clouding her face. She dropped her hand from his arm and stepped away, walking around the seating arrangement toward the dining area in the middle of the large circular building.

As Edin and Margaret reached the dining area, John and Meredith entered from the kitchen side. Meredith squealed and threw herself into Edin's arms, while John greeted his wife with a gentle kiss. He slid his arm around Margaret's shoulders as he turned, smiling, to watch his son swing Meredith around and plant a laughing kiss on her upturned face. Declan smiled. *This family certainly has a thing about swinging each other around.*

Alexandria paused at the back of a tall wing back chair in the great room, sliding one hand back and forth across the forest green damask upholstery, while the other rubbed small circles over her heart. Declan swallowed, his throat tight as he watched. *Why is she so uncertain? What the hell happened to her?*

Declan glided toward Alexandria to offer his presence as comfort before he realized he was even moving.

Meredith launched herself toward Alexandria like a heat-seeking missile, short-circuiting his plan. Before Alexandria could react, she was enveloped in a hug that knocked her back a step. Startled, she belatedly slid her arms around the wiggling Meredith and tentatively returned the hug.

Meredith pulled back. "Oh my God, I'm so sorry, but I was just so excited to meet you. You're so beautiful; the photos Edin has don't do you justice. I'm Meredith. I'm sure Edin's told you nothing. We are going to be..."

As Meredith threw her arms around Alexandria again in a girly version of a bear hug, Declan choked on an abbreviated laugh. The sudden apprehension in Alexandria's eyes stopped him in his tracks. *What is she afraid of?*

Alexandria felt like she was wrestling an octopus; she was being hugged, well, everywhere. Enveloped in a cloud of soft floral scents, she looked down at Edin's girlfriend, who had to be all of five-foot-four. With Meredith's arms wrapped around hers, she was hard-pressed to give a hug back and startled enough to be momentarily speechless.

Meredith's mahogany-brown locks bobble-headed around beneath her chin. Apparently, the girl couldn't stand still. "I'm so happy to meet you, too," Alexandria said.

Meredith stepped back and looked up.

"Damn, you're tall, too. I was hoping someone in this family might be more my size."

Her ear-to-ear grin was infectious, and Alexandria laughed. "Sorry, apparently the tall genes are dominant."

"We can't all have the luck of the gods," Meredith said and turned to Declan. "Well, get over here and give me a hug, you big thug."

Declan obliged and gave her a hug that lifted her off the ground.

"Hey, minx, when are you gonna get smart and ditch Edin for me?"

"Uh, let's see, that would be, never," she replied. She slipped one hand into his and the other into Alexandria's. "Let's eat, I'm starved."

She led them to the table.

Alexandria barely had time to process what had happened before she found herself seated between Meredith and Declan. She looked around the table. Edin was on Meredith's left, then Dad, Margaret, and back around to Declan. No help there, all the allies were distanced from her by the strangers flanking her at the round table.

She wished that the specialized table leaves which expanded the circumference of the table from seating six up to eighteen were in place. Instead, it was at its most compact level, pushing the six of them into close quarters. As she drew her chair closer to the table, her knee bumped Declan's leg and she jumped.

"I don't bite," he said.

"Sorry."

John cleared his throat. "If you two are finished, we'll say grace."

Alexandria bowed her head and tried to ignore the current she felt rolling off of Declan. To her left, Meredith was fidgeting, and she felt hemmed in by foreign energy. She mumbled her 'amen' and looked up to catch her father watching her.

The house staff glided in to serve the first course, a delicious cauliflower and sweet potato soup, served cool with warm bits of fried pancetta as garnish.

Her father lifted his wine glass to make the first toast. "Here's to celebrating the Christmas season with the ones we love..." his glass raised high, he indicated those at the table with the stem end, "to the friends we cherish and the ties of family. May the coming year be blessed for us all."

Glasses clinked among a cacophony of "Salutes" and "Cheers!"

Alexandria sipped her wine and looked at her father and brother. The wine was bitter on her tongue, and anger blazed along her nerve endings, making her heart clench. She set down the glass with a snap. She loved them more than anything in the world and there they sat, so close, yet so far away.

She loved her brother and missed him; his quick wit and open good nature were easy to be around. Five years older, he had paved the way with a ready smile and unending patience when she tagged along with his friends on their adventures. Alexandria stirred the soup with her spoon.

Dad had always been there with a comforting hug and solid advice. Her first camera had been his, handed over in grand tradition. He took her hiking and camping to practice getting her shots.

She loved them and wanted to be a daily part of their lives, but how to manage it? Thoughts churned through her head. They'd always been close, but a few months after Mom died, that had changed thanks to Brent. She couldn't have them without destroying the foundations of their lives. Or could she?

John Marsh knew his daughter well. A lackluster appetite was a sure sign of trouble brewing. He watched her push the delicate sea bass around her plate. Half of her favorite soup had gone back to the kitchen, and the main dish looked destined for the same fate.

Time for some diversion. He caught her eye. "So, what's your latest project?"

"I've been working with the International Sea Turtle Institute out of Tortuguerro, Costa Rica. We followed the turtles through their migratory routes, then through the egg laying and hatching."

Edin broke in, "You watched giant turtles do the nasty?"

Alexandria slanted him a sideways look. "Better them than you."

Meredith choked on her wine. Alexandria graciously pounded on her back, maybe with a little too much enthusiasm to make up for her earlier blasé hug.

"Did you actually swim with the turtles?" Margaret directed the conversation back to a safer ground.

"Not so much swimming as diving. I learned to dive in high school but got my Surface Supplied Air Diver card and Master Diver certification three years ago for the Barrier Reef gig with NatGeo." As Declan leaned closer, Alexandria scooted left.

John could feel the energy between them from across the table.

Declan looked directly into her eyes, "So, you've deep dived with giant sea turtles, chased sharks and whales, provided expedition photo-journaling for volcanologists in Iceland, and yet, you turn down a very lucrative contract for the Kukenam Tepui expedition?"

Alexandria opened her mouth but snapped it shut. *What the blazes?*

Declan sounded pissed, like a child denied his favorite toy. More importantly, how the hell did he know about that? She glanced from him to Edin, who shrugged. "Yes. Exactly what business would that be of yours?"

"Entirely mine, as it's my expedition. I've seen your work

and wanted that level of quality for this trip. I told Hank to hire you. He said he couldn't."

Thought of months spent in close proximity with Declan warmed her cheeks. The flush of warmth was spreading to other places, too. A pang of regret stabbed her. "I couldn't commit...I'm sorry." How could she tell him that, despite the strong attraction to the project, the moment she saw the letterhead from Edin's law firm and Brent's signature, she had turned it down flat?

Margaret passed a basket of rolls to her right. "John was telling me your family is in pharmaceuticals?"

"Yes. My great-grandfather founded the company," Declan replied. "Our emphasis is on nature-based chemistry, so we invest in significant field research. That's my specialty, or was, until running the company took priority."

"But we've got that squared away now," Edin said, "and you can get back in the field where you belong."

"Well, you two can discuss your expedition while Alexandria gives you the grand tour tomorrow." Five sets of startled eyes looked at Margaret. "He needs a tour, and the rest of us are occupied tomorrow. For tonight, we're catching up. It's been too long since we've had the family together." She smiled at both Declan and Meredith. "And if you're wondering, you're included in the family if you're on this island with us at Christmas."

CHAPTER SIX

The scents of jasmine, freesia, and plumeria danced on cool evening breezes that ruffled the pale green silk sheers.

Alexandria curled her legs under her, nestling into the corner of the French Roll armchair. Its soft jade and gold upholstery caressed her skin wherever it touched her, and in turn she ran her hand tenderly over the arm. She loved the house's great room, always had, with its soothing decor in shades of green, brown and gold. With the great glass doors open it felt like an extension of the jungle, just more comfortable. As she watched the moonrise through the open patio doors, she sipped her cappuccino. Bing crooned his wishes for a white Christmas softly in the background and Alexandria smiled. Some things just didn't fit together.

But then again, some things did. Edin sat on the over-sized chaise with Meredith on his lap where they seemed to be in perfect harmony. Meredith's affectionate energy was infectious and intensified Alexandria's happiness for her brother.

Even Declan, lounging in the matching armchair with

his head leaning back and his flip flops abandoned on the floor, seemed to be exactly right. With his long legs stretched out before him and his left hand swirling his snifter of eighteen-year-old Glenmorangie, he appeared quite content.

She smiled into her cup but glanced up as John and Margaret pushed a teak tea cart in from the kitchen. Her interest piqued; Alexandria straightened. A platter of mouth-watering Scottish Shortbread and Italian Christmas cookies dominated the cart. But, as Margaret stopped the cart in the center of the room, the lump in Alex's throat had nothing to do with cookies. She stared at the Spode bone china tea set covered with Christmas roses. She tore her eyes away to look at Edin, who was also staring at the teapot, and turned her gaze to Margaret.

Margaret hesitated, and John smiled his encouragement, his hand on the small of her back. She looked from Alexandria to Edin and back to Alex. "This day, of all the days we know, is so much about family. Too much time has passed since we were all together, and it wouldn't be right to be here without the presence of our beloved Caterina."

Alexandria stared at her mother's Christmas Rose teapot for a long moment. Setting her coffee cup aside, she rose and gave Margaret a fierce hug.

Margaret held her tight, her voice a soft whisper in Alex's ear. "I miss her too, honey." Releasing Alexandria she motioned to the cart. "Care to do the honors?"

Alexandria raised both hands in protest. "No, but thanks. Mom would roll over in her grave to hear me clanking her precious teapot about."

John laughed and threw his arm around his daughter, pulling her in close. "You were always a little rough with things that break."

From the safety of her father's arms she stuck her tongue out when Edin laughed. Kissing the top of her head he released her and she snuggled back in her comfy armchair.

Margaret had already dished up dainty plates of cookies and was handing them out. She served the hot spiced tea just as efficiently, and soon the sounds of sipping tea and crunching cookies mingled with laughter and jovial conversation.

Alexandria savored the shortbread on her tongue. *How could anyone not love love love such buttery, sugary delight?* Her eyes closed in bliss until a wadded napkin hit her square in the face. "Ahk!" She opened her eyes and glared at her heathen brother.

"What are you doing over there, sis? Getting your O face on?" Edin laughed hard until Meredith smacked him on the back of the head.

She glared at him. "And you wonder why I haven't hung out with you for four years?"

Edin instantly sobered. "Hey, I'm..."

Alexandria cut him off with a laugh. "Gotcha, weasel bag."

"Weasel bag?" Declan snorted as Edin relaxed back with a smile. "Where did you learn to fight?"

"Mom was adamant that well-behaved young ladies didn't curse or call names, at least ones of a certain type—so Al made up her own. Mom just never realized that Al wasn't well behaved." Edin answered.

"Really? What else is in the repertoire?" Declan asked.

Alexandria leaned forward.

"Guys, guys, settle down," Her Daddy came to her defense. "It's Christmas Eve, be nice. Besides, some time-honored Marsh traditions are in order."

"Uh, Dad, we're a little old for the pull-my-finger gag." Edin rolled his eyes and waggled his index finger.

At the insulted look on John's face, laughter erupted. Margaret snuggled against John on the love-seat they shared. John looked to Declan and Meredith. "When Caterina was with us, every Christmas we would each share something we were grateful for in the year we left behind us and declare something we wanted to achieve in the next year."

"Awesome. In fact, I'm thinking I'll go first with this one." Edin stood and took Meredith's hand to pull her up beside him, his arm curling around her shoulders. He glanced at his dad. "I know Dad is beyond grateful that my beautiful and annoying sister is with us this year, and I agree with him wholeheartedly."

Guilt warmed Alexandria cheeks.

"But I have to say that what I am most grateful for this year is that this little Tasmanian devil--" Edin looked at the woman at his side and back to the group--"Meredith Thaxton, spitfire, neo-natal nurse extraordinaire and holder of my heart," he smiled, "has agreed to be my wife."

Declan and Alexandria gasped.

Alexandria bounded from her chair to throw her arms around Edin's neck and squeeze him tight. "I'm so happy for you, for both of you." She turned from Edin to envelop Meredith in a hug. Meredith's breath left her in a huff.

"Hey, can't breathe here, sis."

Alexandria relaxed her hug but couldn't contain her happiness. She smiled at her sister-in-law to be. "I can't believe it. I never thought Edin would lose his heart. Are you sure he's worthy of you?"

A loud snort and a swat at her behind were Edin's reply.

But Meredith pulled her out of harm's way and stuck out her tongue at Edin. "He tries hard not to be some days, but he's not gonna get away that easy."

Longing to belong somewhere brought Declan to his feet, despite feeling like a gatecrasher as he watched the family cluster together. He made his way to Edin, giving him a congratulatory back-pounding. "Man, that's great. You're a lucky bastard."

Edin headed toward the bar with Declan in tow. "Glad you think so, because I want you at my back—as my best man."

Declan's raised his brows. "Me, the purveyor of no strings, no ties?"

Edin shrugged with an awkward grin. He glanced out the open patio doors and back. "You're a damn fine friend, dating philosophies aside." He grinned. "I can't think of anyone I would be more honored to have stand by me."

As John ambled over, Edin poured them each two fingers of Glenmorangie neat. He tossed a small splash of water in each glass of finely aged whiskey and lifted his glass in a toast as each man did the same.

Raising his glass in salute, Declan swallowed the lump in his throat. "Honored to be asked." Edin's and John's glasses raised to his. "Honored to serve. Honored to be your friend."

Glasses clinked, and the sweet fire of whiskey sealed the bonds.

As John moved toward the men, Margaret joined Meredith and Alexandria.

About five seconds after pulling Meredith down close beside her on the couch, Alexandria's mind caught up with her heart. *Engagement equals wedding equates to guests, so what do I do?* Despite her darkening thoughts, she continued to smile.

Margaret pounced on the opposite side. "This is so exciting."

Alexandria looked at her stepmother. "But you already knew, didn't you?"

A knowing smile softened Margaret's reproach. "Secrets entrusted, intentionally or otherwise, are sacred. If you gave your father and me a secret to carry, you wouldn't want it exposed until you were ready. Edin and Mere wanted to tell you themselves."

Alexandria had the good grace to blush.

Meredith grinned. "She's right. We wanted to tell you and we didn't want it to be right up in your face, gee you're back, guess what."

Alexandria smiled at her. "So, we're going to be sisters. Having a sister used to be my birthday wish, especially seeing how Edin is such a pain in the ass."

Meredith laughed. "Me, too. I've always wanted a family. So, in my mind, I'm kinda marrying you all."

Both women squeezed her between them and kissed her cheeks.

Margaret laughed. "You might be rethinking that after a few years in the family."

Alexandria sat back, only to catch Margaret watching her with a speculative gleam in her eyes. Still holding Meredith's hand, her fingers felt numb and tingly, while her palms were starting to sweat. Meredith was a nurse and would certainly notice that, wouldn't she? What was Margaret thinking? That woman was way too observant. Too bad she wasn't in the law enforcement game. There would be no unsolved crimes.

Alexandria forced herself to refocus. "I guess big plans are in order for the coming year?" she asked. "Have you set a date?"

Meredith looked her square in the eyes. "Well, yes, we have, and almost everything is all set."

"Wow, you're pretty efficient. Or I'm really the last to know." Alexandria couldn't help but feel *very* left out.

"Maybe both. But one critical component missing." A shy smile bloomed. "I know you just met me, but I would so very much like you to be my maid of honor, and I wanted to be the one to ask you."

Meredith's warm aura drew her in. Tears welled in Alexandria's eyes, and she clasped Meredith close. "Meredith, I don't know what to say. Of course, I'll be there for you." In her mind, her options churned but one mantra repeated. *There has to be a way.*

Margaret squealed in delight. "Tell her the rest!"

Alexandria leaned away from Meredith. "The rest? You're not planning to marry me off, too, are you?"

Meredith laughed at her new sister-to-be. "No silly, just the plans."

Her warm smile soothed Alexandria's frayed nerves.

"I've no family to speak of and we want a simple, quiet wedding."

Alexandria's heart raced. Could it be? Would she get off this easily? Her lips quirked in a one-sided smile. "Define simple and quiet."

"New Year's Day, here. How's that?"

"As in seven days from now?"

"That would be it."

Alexandria's smile felt bigger than her face. "Where do we start?"

CHAPTER SEVEN

Margaret walked out of the bathroom of their suite and paused.

John stood deep in thought, staring out the floor-to-ceiling glass facing the wide Pacific Ocean.

She could tell from the set of his shoulders that none of the breathtaking scenery was making its way into his thoughts. She went to him, slid her arms around his waist, and laid her cheek against his back. "What is it?"

"I don't want to lose her."

"She's here, and that's more than we've had with her in a long time."

"I know, but she's not herself, and there's something between her and Declan. We moved mountains to get her here, and I don't want Declan screwing it up."

She laughed. "What is rolling off them in waves is mutual attraction, and both of them are determined to ignore it, discount it, or otherwise explain it away."

Her embrace loosened, and he turned in her arms. His hands slid up and down her back, the soft silk of her negligée whispering against her skin. Soft scents of freesia floated in the air and he took a deep breath, laying his cheek on the top of her head. "Meggie, he's a decent guy, but this is my little girl. He's not the kind a father hopes his daughter will bring home. He has a rep. And she's so stiff and uptight, I could use her as a surfboard. She used to be so full of joy. Nothing ruffled her."

Margaret took his face in her hands, forcing eye contact. "They are both good people and they've been hurt. I can feel it. They are fully armored right now and using all their defenses to keep people away from their hearts. If they are attracted to each other enough to get past that kind of armament, you won't be able to stop it."

His hands pulled hers from his face to trap them between them. "You're not...matchmaking...are you?"

She pulled free and sashayed toward the bed. Glancing over her shoulder, she smiled. "Don't be silly. I'm just ensuring everyone gets what they need to have a fabulous Christmas."

CHAPTER EIGHT

The excitement of Christmas morning never dimmed for Alexandria. She hurried into the great room, where dozens of gifts nestled under an eight-foot noble pine covered with gold and red decorations. Large, hand-blown glass ornaments reflected the warm glow of hundreds of twinkling lights. Grinning she softly tapped several gold bells hung on the branches. "Another angel gets her wings," she whispered.

"At the rate you're going, another legion or two will be joining the ranks."

Startled, Alexandria turned to find Declan at her side. His strong hand reached out and deftly flicked two bells in quick succession.

He grinned. "I get to contribute, too, you know."

She tapped another bell. "I love Christmas."

"So I've heard." Declan's smile was warm and gentle like the breeze coming through the open deck doors.

"See this one?" She pointed to a glass globe painted with a scene of Santa in his workshop. "My mom and I bought this one at the Vienna Christmas markets."

"It's beautiful, full of joy, like you and your mother."

Alexandria looked at him in surprise.

He shrugged. "I've seen your mother's picture. A black-and-white shot near some glacier."

"Portage Glacier in Alaska. I took it."

"It's in Edin's office. Gorgeous shot, by the way. Even in black-and-white, you captured her joy of life."

Alexandria's eyes misted; her throat tightened. She tapped bells with a light rhythm, turning her head away to look out the doors to the sea beyond.

"You miss her a lot."

Alexandria nodded, even though it wasn't a question. She took a deep breath and turned back. "What about you? Up early and here at the tree? Elf or eager little boy?" she teased. When he smiled, her mood lightened.

"No pointy ears," he said in amusement, "and a little hairy to classify as a boy, but I'm usually up early. It was a beautiful sunrise."

As she watched him run his thumb along the stubble on his jawline her mouth went dry.

"I know. I love the dawn. A bright new day. A new beginning...." Her voice trailed off. *Stop blathering.*

"If I'd known you were a dawn fan, we could've admired it together over a nice coffee."

Visions of him, warm, naked and snuggled against her as a golden yellow sun climbed through purple pre-dawn clouds raced fast forward through her mind. Alexandria flushed and stared at his mouth. Deep in her abdomen the moist heat of desire bloomed.

"You do drink coffee?"

The question broke her trance. The heat in her cheeks deepened, and she cleared her throat.

"Sure, but I prefer tea, usually."

"How do you feel about breakfast in bed?"

"You two are up early!" Edin's voice sliced the space between them.

Alexandria stepped back; she hadn't realized they had gravitated together until they were nearly touching as they had talked.

Edin, with Meredith in tow, entered the great room from the hallway that connected the family's private quarters.

As she caught Edin's pointed look at Declan, who just barely shrugged his shoulders in response, Alexandria's eyes narrowed.

"Merry Christmas!" rang through the room as they greeted each other and the day.

Alexandria hugged Edin, then glided away toward Meredith. She looked more asleep than awake. Alexandria led her to the sideboard.

"Coffee?"

"Oh, yes." Meredith yawned widely. "You people are way too perky for this time of day. I don't care if it is Christmas."

"Cream? Sugar?"

Meredith nodded to both. Alexandria shoved the mug into Meredith's hands and guided her to the love seat.

"Now that we're sisters, you're my new partner in crime. Mom and I used to drive Dad and Edin nuts at Christmas, so you're gonna have to rise to the occasion."

"I'm on board with the driving nuts part, but do we have to do it so early?" Meredith complained with a sleepy smile.

As Alexandria watched Edin deep in conversation with Declan by the tree, her heart tightened. She caught Edin's indulgent smile. She gave him her best mischievous grin in return, which, to her childish delight, put a definite note of concern on Edin's face. Turning back to Meredith, she made her offer. "I'll let you sleep in the other three hundred sixty-four if you give me Christmas."

Meredith laughed. "Deal."

John and Margaret swept in from the kitchen. Another chorus of Christmas greetings echoed through the room. Everyone converged near the tree and, amid hugs and Christmas kisses, Alexandria found herself turned from Margaret's arms into Declan's embrace. His warm lips touched her temple in a gentle kiss. Her pulse pounding, she breathed deep, but his warm, earthy scent didn't aid in regaining her composure.

"Merry Christmas! Who's ready for presents?" John's booming voice filled the room.

Alexandria turned away from Declan and pounced on her father and Margaret, hugging and kissing them while she dragged them closer to the tree, her readiness all too apparent.

Breakfast was an informal affair with the buffet being set up on the sideboard. The scents of bacon and sausage blended with the spicy tang of cinnamon. Bowls of fresh fruits shared space with warm coffeecakes and delicate quiches.

Her plate laden with things too good to resist, Alexandria again found herself between Meredith and Declan. While she still felt the heat of his attraction, she no longer felt confined by their energy.

Meredith was bringing her up to speed on how she'd met Edin when Alexandria heard Margaret ask Declan about his family's Christmas traditions. A hand on Meredith's arm to pause her, she turned to catch his reply. Her right hand caressed the new silver Celtic cross lying over her heart.

"We don't have any now."

"None?" she blurted.

Declan's lips quirked and he shook his head.

Margaret sipped her coffee. "How do your parents celebrate?" She turned to fix her gaze on Edin. "You should have invited his parents."

Edin opened his mouth, but Declan spoke first.

"Mom passed away when I was fourteen." He glanced at Alexandria, then turned back to Margaret. "She loved Christmas and always made it extra special. Dad's never had any interest in celebrating since."

Compassion filled Margaret's gentle brown eyes. "I'm sorry. I didn't mean to dredge up unhappy memories."

"It's fine. It was a long time ago."

John inclined his head towards Alexandria. "Sounds like she would've been a good fit with my Caterina and Al here. They always took it to a whole new level."

"I'm sure they would have." Declan's gaze was tender as he looked into Alexandria's eyes.

The surge of emotion sweeping through Declan was dangerous, and he knew it. Alexandria's eyes were pools of deep forest green. He could lose himself in their depths, not to mention how deep he'd like to be inside the rest of her.

Her nearness raised the fine hairs on his forearms, and his cock was throbbing. Meredith's conversation had kept her occupied most of the meal, but everything about her filled his senses. As he watched her fingers stroke the silver Celtic Unity cross he had given her earlier, he found himself jealous of the cold metal lying on the swell of her breast.

Watching her unwrap the cross earlier, exclaiming and excited to put it on, had been hard enough. Never one to arrive empty-handed, Declan had easily enough procured gifts for everyone but her. Something just right for a mysterious sister had eluded him until he saw the finely wrought cross in the Gaelic store in Chicago's The Shops at North Bridge Mall.

He'd been heading to Nordstrom's when wind-driven sleet had detoured him inside the tiny shop. Browsing the displays to avoid the curious clerk, he'd been ready to leave when it caught his eye. The elegant weaving of Celtic Trinity knots had given him a strange sense of déjà vu that just felt right. Until he'd gotten back to his office and glanced at the photo of his mother on his desk and the Celtic cross she always wore that he made the connection. She'd never been without the cross that his dad had fastened around her neck on their first official date. After that, writing off the feelings as remembered familiarity was easy enough.

Now, as it lay there at the edge of Alexandria's bodice, teasing him, he wanted to kiss her warm, golden skin and suckle her nipples into tight buds of heated desire. He shifted in his seat, refocusing his thoughts. She was deep in conversation with Meredith. Declan turned toward Edin.

"So, what's the plan for today? Do I have time before you lay the best man duties on me?" Declan asked.

The deep timbre of Declan's voice drew Alexandria's attention more than the words. She looked between the two men but concentrated on Edin. The heat coming off Declan could fuel a small village, and she needed to be distracted before she did something stupid.

Edin smiled at Alexandria and gave an apologetic shrug. "I know Al likes to celebrate the day *all day,* but we've no snow for snowmen. Besides which, Mere and Margaret have Dad and me up to our ears in "To Do's" before we get to the "I Do's."

Declan nodded towards Alexandria. "Anything we can help with?"

Edin shook his head.

"As I mentioned last night, we've got our hands full today and I expect Alexandria to give you a tour." Margaret took matters in hand. "We may not be big enough to get permanently lost on, but we've plenty of interesting sights. If she tours you today, you'll have plenty of time to explore at your leisure later."

"But we could help today and there'd be plenty of time to explore tomorrow," Alexandria said.

Edin cleared his throat. "Not actually." He put his hand up to forestall Declan. "I promised you peace and quiet and you'll have it. Mere and I have to go to Saipan Wednesday and Thursday to pick up guests..."

"Guests?" Alexandria's voice squeaked and she choked on her orange juice.

Declan shifted to thump her on the back and his thigh touched hers. Tension clenched her quadriceps and with his leg pressed to hers, she knew he felt it.

Although he returned his attention to Edin, she knew he watched her from the corner of his eye.

"Yeah, guests. We might not want a big wedding, but we want some of our friends share this occasion with us."

"As in?" she asked.

"You remember Rudy and Leann. Then there's Tom and Rosamund Greenley."

Alexandria nodded.

Edin glanced at Meredith as if seeking reassurance. "Victor Tamblin and his current girl, I think her name is Lucy—and Brent."

"Brent! You invited Brent?" Alexandria pushed back from the table and fled to the patio doors. She braced her hand on the jam and stared, unseeing, at the scenery beyond. Her mind was numb, a myriad of coherent thoughts swirled in her mind but wouldn't settle into usable order. A rising panic made her want to abandon all pretense and shoot across the deck and into the jungle. At least, she knew how to handle the predators in there.

Before she could react, Edin's arm came around her shoulders, pulling her close to his side.

"C'mon," he said, moving out to the deck. He squeezed her shoulder.

She looked at him but turned her face away.

"I'm sorry, E," Alexandria said. "Of course, you'd want guests, and he's your best friend."

Edin gave her a lame smile. "I wouldn't say my BFF, but a friend, and my partner at the firm." At the far side of the pool, he turned her to face him and slid his hands down her arms to take her hands in his.

"Honey, it's been four years, and you *dumped* him."

She opened her mouth to speak, but he put his finger on her lips to silence her before taking her hand again.

"Please let me finish. You left. You never talk about him, and I figured he was, well, a non-issue for you. I can't change that now. Dad and I have been so afraid. After Mom..." Edin swallowed hard and looked away. He brought his gaze back to hers. "After Mom died, you started avoiding us; we felt like we had lost you both. It hurt so fucking bad, and we won't lose you again. I'll turn Brent around at the airport."

The realization that her cure was worse than the disease hit her so hard she lost her breath. "Edin, I'm so sorry." Her arms went around his waist, and she laid her cheek on his broad chest. *All these years, I thought I was protecting you. All these years with you and Dad, lost. I have to fix this.*

A lone tear slid down her cheek, and she lifted a game smile to Edin. "Please don't change any of the plans you've made. You're right; it's been a long time. I'm sure he doesn't care one way or the other." The lie slid easily from her lips.

"I'd turn him around a thousand times a day if it would put a smile on your face."

"The tears aren't for him or about him, they're for you. I never meant to hurt you and Dad. Please forgive me."

Edin kissed her forehead and pulled her close. "We're good, just never leave us like that again."

His deep voice reverberated through her. "Deal." Alexandria couldn't let Edin know *just* how much Brent would care. She thought of all the texts, emails, and voice-mails she had deleted without response over the last four years. She would find a way.

Alexandria stopped at the edge of the corridor. Declan was standing overlooking the pool and the sea beyond. With his back to her, she was able to observe him at her leisure. To say he set her teeth on edge was an understatement. With Brent's imminent arrival looming on the horizon like an F-5 shit storm, the last thing she needed was distraction in the form of one Declan Ruaidhrí. Never mind that he was only man who had ever made her lose coherent thought to the point she just wanted to jump him.

Sapphire blue board shorts set off his deep tan and the black muscle tee emphasized his broad shoulders. Everything about the man appealed to her most basic instincts. He was dangerous to her heart. Even now, the warmth of attraction spread through her limbs with a languid rush of early desire. When he looked at her and his eyes softened from their cold gunmetal blue to a soft gray that enveloped her like mist in the forest, her resolve melted.

Alexandria gave herself a mental shakedown. Steeling her emotions, she tossed her backpack over her shoulder, sliding her other arm into its strap. Never one to shirk a duty, she walked resolutely out the patio doors.

CHAPTER NINE

Alexandria's particular perfume of jasmine and sunshine hit Declan before she cleared the patio doors. He took a deep breath and wished his resolve to keep her at a distance was as steely as his cock, which was currently turning his nice loose board shorts into the Barnum big top. He let his backpack slip partly off his shoulder and in front to help hide the damning evidence of his desire. At the sound of her soft voice, he turned his head.

"You ready for the Grand Tour?" she asked.

"Yep. Lead the way, my liege."

"You must be gender confused. I'm the wrong sex for a liege lord."

A soft snort escaped Declan as he fell in behind her on the trail that led off the pool deck. He definitely wasn't gender confused. At least, behind her she wouldn't notice he was sporting wood to rival any of the bamboo along the trail. His intent gaze took her in from bottom to top, which did nothing to help the situation in his shorts.

Her black, well-worn Keen all-terrain sandals emphasized her long, golden legs—well-muscled in a way that spoke of a healthy, active life. Unlike the fashion-conscious social climbers who usually crossed his path. They'd run a pedestrian over for the chance to park as close as possible to the yoga studio. Marching up the trail into an ever-denser sea of green, he was mesmerized by the rhythm those legs provided to the absolutely gorgeous ass they carried. The deep green khaki cargo shorts were fitted just enough for him to appreciate the scenery of her sway and the curve of her hips.

He could just imagine the view from the front. She was wearing a loose, button-front, jungle shirt over a white tank. The scoop neck emphasized the swell of luscious breasts, full and perfectly sized for her height and build. Her long, beautiful curls were braided and twisted into a bundle at the back of her head, secured by a giant clip thing. A few soft tendrils had escaped their confinement and were curling against her neck. Her backpack had a couple of small rips and patches, and he even found its obvious wear and tear sexy. He was so totally screwed. *I am going to fucking kill Edin. Right after the wedding.*

Thoroughly engrossed in his observations, he hardly registered his surroundings. He barely avoided being swatted in the face by a branch she pushed aside in their progress up the trail. Ah hell, she was talking. "Sorry, I couldn't catch that."

She stopped abruptly and half turned to him. She gave him a oddball look like he had lost his mind and pointed off the trail toward towering trees. "Howler monkeys at 10:00, fifty degrees high. You know, 12:00 in front of you, 6:00 behind you, 90 degrees above you...."

"Yeah, I get it, I just didn't hear you." Declan's peevish tone earned him a dirty look, and feeling like a dumb ass didn't sit well with him. He focused on the monkeys in the trees, trying to get his composure back. At least, the steady trail climb and feeling like a dumb shit had calmed the storm in his pants.

She shrugged and took off, her pace a little faster than before. Stuffing aside his irritation, he focused on anything and everything on the trail except the woman he followed. He kept up easily but when she came to an abrupt stop on a widened area of the path he nearly bumped into her.

She turned with a finger to her lips, signaling him to silence.

He moved beside her. The trail curved sharply to the right and started a heavy climb. The sounds of tumbling, splashing water mingled with odd plopping noises and chattering. They crept along the curve of the high slope. Alexandria crouched down with Declan looming over her.

On the opposite slope from the path, a gurgling stream cascaded over a rocky outcropping creating a fifteen-foot waterfall into a lovely pool bounded by large rocks on the path side. The wide pool filled the natural basin before gracefully exiting between two Purple Mangosteen trees on its path to the sea. The bubbling water near the falls subsided midway across into a silent, smooth surface reflecting puffy white clouds and the jungle tree line.

A handful of tall macadamia trees graced the opposite bank and three spider monkeys teased a small, gray bettong washing its paws on the bank, excitedly chattering and tossing nut shells. The beauty of the sheltered pool took Declan's breath away. He crouched closer to Alexandria, his mouth close to her ear and his hand resting lightly on her shoulder. "Amazing."

She nodded slightly. "My second favorite place on the island." Whispering softly she glanced aside at him.

A distant sound intruded on the scene and both the

bettong and the monkeys fled into the jungle. Declan rose to his full height, his hand under Alexandria's elbow as she stood. "If this is your second, I can't wait to see the first."

"It may not live up to your expectations. This pool is gorgeous. I love to come up here for a cool swim." She blushed softly. "Before you ask, yes, I've skinny-dipped here. I think everyone has, at some point."

His deep laugh felt good as it chased away his earlier irritation. "Good to know. Maybe we'll come back some evening." He waggled his brows.

She laughed at his humor.

"We'll see. You might find you like some other place better. Quick checkpoint for you." She gestured back the way they came and swept her hand in the up-trail direction. "We're on the main trail that runs pretty much up the center of the island. It starts off on the north side of the pool. This trail is the best maintained and used most often to move up island. It leads straight up to the north cliffs."

"There are others?"

"Two. One that starts down by the harbor and follows the shoreline, but it meanders and takes a while. We'll go back that way. The other starts from behind the family wing of the house. It's narrow and sometimes dangerous where it follows the cliff edge up, but it's the shortest and fastest, if you're in a hurry."

"How far to the cliffs?"

"The whole trail is about an hour. We're about twenty minutes into it." As Alexandria started up the trail, Declan fell in beside her. She had an intriguing voice, the soft, husky timbre of it stroked his mind like silk sliding over his skin. She was easy to listen to and he was impressed. She could give any flora and fauna guide he knew a run for their money. Her knowledge of the island habitats wasn't limited to the kinds and types but their medicinal purposes and alternate uses. "Do you know what I do?"

As she glanced at him, she quirked her eyebrow. "Actually, no. I'm sorry. I should have asked."

"Considering this is the most personal conversation we've had, I wouldn't have expected you to know. I not sure what details were included in the expedition offer."

"The letter just laid out the timing and expectations of the work scope. Purpose wasn't included. When your guy called me, it didn't come up." She smiled sheepishly. "I kinda cut him off."

"Maybe you'll reconsider before our time here is through."

Her smile didn't quite reach her eyes. "Maybe."

Part of him desperately wanted to push her to reconsider now, but his intuition pulled him up short. Whatever was going on with her self-exile from her family had something to do with why she wouldn't accept his offer. He decided in that moment to figure it out.

Approaching the summit, the trail broadened. Beneath their feet, an enormous granite promontory spread in both directions. The lush growth of the jungle stopped abruptly at its edge, but curved around the sides, determined surround the rock formation. Its rough, uneven surface held small pockets of dirt and even tiny bits of growing plants, but its sheer size and lack of cracks made it all but uninhabitable by even the island's smallest flora.

A handful of boulders were strewn about, particularly closer to the drop off. As Alexandria marched over and chose one for a perch, Declan's stomach did an odd little flop. He swallowed his desire to caution her and instead let his feet lead him to the southeastern side of the bluff. As he neared where the jungle ploughed up to and over the edge, he saw the narrow opening of a trail. He pointed and called to Alexandria. "The fast trail?"

She nodded.

He turned back to her, walking along the cliff. Trying to gauge the immensity of the stone beneath his feet. It appeared to be one enormous formation, which would account for its stability over time. However, below him, thousands of pounds of rock lying in broken and scattered shapes were taking a pounding from the surge of the Pacific Ocean. As each surge pressed against the island's bulk, spray flung high into the air.

He walked back to her and sat down on a nearby rock. She was drinking from her canteen and as he watched the smooth skin of her throat move in rhythm with her swallows, his mouth went dry. Small beads of moisture from the climb and the warm, late morning sun glistened on her skin. He wanted to lick them off her.

She offered the canteen.

He took a number of quick swallows and handed it back. Setting his pack on a boulder, he opened it and pulled out two protein bars and two bananas. "Hungry?" He offered her first choice.

"Thanks," she said, grinning. "Nice to know you packed well." She selected a banana and a cranberry-almond bar.

"I do have my moments of pure genius."

They both laughed and ate in silence, listening to the pounding of the surf.

Declan broke the silence. "So, when do I get to see your favorite place on the island?"

Looking askance at him, she turned back to the wide Pacific Ocean vista. "I thought maybe we'd finish the tour and I'd make you guess."

"Hm, sounds like a good plan, except I think we're

already at your favorite place." He swept his arm out to encompass the view of the horizon. "I think the power and solitude of this place would be at the top of your list."

Alexandria started in surprise. *How is it this virtual stranger can see in me what my family can't understand or accept?* Frustration with her family made her answer sharper than she intended. "How'd you guess?"

A frown marred his handsome features.

She tried to backtrack. "I'm sorry. That was much ruder sounding than I meant. Actually, I didn't mean to be rude at all. I was so surprised."

Declan fished his iPhone from his pocket to snap a panoramic shot of the sea. "Are you always rude when you're surprised?"

"No, well, I never used to be." She looked off into the distance. But then she looked back and laughed. "Either way I answer that, I sound awful. Either I've always been rude, or I just started."

He stared out at the sea. "So, what happened?"

A cold vise squeezed her heart. Her hands fumbled as she shoved her canteen back in the side pouch of her pack. She stood up abruptly, but before she could move, Declan was there in front of her. His hands on her shoulders. The concern in his eyes pleaded for explanation, but she had no words. Her mouth opened. Nothing came out.

"Whoa, Al," he whispered. His thumbs caressed her collar-bones, feather-light, but heat coursed over her skin, her breasts tingled, and her nipples puckered into hard nubs. Her pack slipped unnoticed to the ground, her hands came up to rest on his chest, to feel his heat, his strength.

His right hand slide down her shoulder blade to her waist, where he pulled her close. His left moved up the column of her neck, his fingers rustling her hair. The soft movements sending pins of sensation through her soul and waves of emotion flooding her body.

His blue-gray eyes were turbulent, like the skies after a wild storm.

Alexandria couldn't, wouldn't look away. As his lips covered hers, her eyes slid closed. His warm mouth pressed gently against her own, a soft moan escaped her, and she leaned into him. Gliding her hands to his back, pulling him closer, she felt a tremor in his muscles.

His lips slid from hers, to her cheekbone, to her temple, to the curve of her brow and were gone.

"Oh, Al, shush."

At his words, her protest died on her lips.

"Let's have this moment, shall we?" He tucked her against him, her cheek on his warm, broad chest. His arms enclosing her in a cocoon of strength. She relaxed against him, and they stood entwined, watching the sea.

The tension and anxiety of the last four years hammered at her, like the pounding of surf against the rocks below, determined to wear her down. As he rubbed her back lightly, the knot of tension coiled like a viper and suddenly she was sick of carrying it with her. Sick of enabling this vile cycle to continue. A lone tear escaped her, only to be caught on the tip of Declan's finger. His lips kissed away its tracks.

"Al, I'm sorry. I didn't mean to upset you, and I shouldn't have kissed you. I don't want to hurt you. I just..." Declan paused, uncertain, "I was trying to give you the chance to talk. I'll listen."

She trembled but looked up at him. "I want to talk. I just

don't know what to say, or where to start."

He guided her to a large rock that would accommodate them both. They sat, her thigh against the length of his leg with his arm around her. His concern confused her. *If he was sorry he kissed her, why was he being so kind?*

He smiled. "Before you start, I'll ask you to keep a confidence."

She nodded her agreement.

"Our kiss? If you tell Edin he'll kill me. Maybe your dad, too. Edin told me to keep my hands off you and your dad hasn't said as much, but I get the same vibes from him."

Alexandria's eyes widened. "Excuse me. *They* don't want you to touch me?"

At Declan's nod, Alexandria threw her head back and laughed, a bitter, angry laugh. "Well, don't worry. Your secret is safe. I don't want your blood on my hands. But don't any of you think I should maybe have some say in just who the hell I fucking choose to kiss?"

He opened his mouth to respond but snapped it shut.

"First, they force me to come here, and now, they are puppeteering my life. Holy shit."

He grabbed her hand. "Stop it. It's not you. It's me. They wanted to protect you."

"Why? Are you going to hurt me?" Regret, and something else, showed in his eyes.

He looked into the distance.

Alexandria took a couple of deep breaths to calm herself.

He turned to look at her, a wry smile on his lips. "I am not a long term kinda guy. I don't get involved with anyone who doesn't know up front that I won't commit to any kind of relationship. They both know that."

"Oh." Her response sounded small, even to her. "Why?"

His look was searing, and his jaw tightened so that she heard teeth grind.

His right hand fisted before he ran it down his thigh and leaned forward to balance his elbows on the tops of his knees. He intertwined the fingers of his hands and looked over his shoulder at her. "I guess it's only fair that if I'm sitting here asking you to spill whatever it is that eats at you, that you could ask the same."

She started to deny his statement, but he glanced away and spoke so that she had to strain to catch his words.

"I was engaged once. She was beautiful, and I was besotted." He glanced back with a quirky smile. "People don't use that word much, I guess. But I was a fool for her, right up to the day I found out she was fucking one of my competitors." He turned his face back to the wide Pacific. "I guess she was sizing us up, to see who would provide the best lifestyle and what bennies were in it for her. I walked out and never looked back."

His bitterness filled her. She leaned her cheek against his shoulder, her right arm laid across his back with her hand on the back of his neck and her left on his bicep. "I'm so sorry, Declan, that's awful."

"I felt used, and I've made a point to not let anyone use me since. I've done the using, which makes me someone your family doesn't want you to be involved with, and they're right."

Declan stared at the sea in shocked disbelief. He had just exposed his darkest hour to a woman he barely knew. The ugly truth that mocked him at every turn was in her hands. A weapon to destroy what little heart he had left. He had locked those remnants away, determined no cold-hearted bitch would ever hurt him again.

"I know how you feel." Alexandria's tremulous voice barely broke a whisper.

"I doubt that."

"It's why I left."

He turned to stare at her. "What?"

"That's why I left."

Alexandria's luminous green eyes looked straight at him and burrowed into his heart.

"My mom died four years ago, in the summer. She was everything to me—my mom, my friend, my confidante." A wan smile curved her lips. "I was lost without her, but I had Dad and Edin...and Brent."

She lowered her gaze to where her fingers were twisting together in lap. "I met Brent when I was in college. He worked with Edin at the firm and we all moved in the same social circles. He was the epitome of tall, dark, and handsome. I just didn't realize the dark went deeper than his looks."

Declan watched her, this beautiful, passionate woman, and realized all he wanted was to see her smile again. He cleared his throat. "You don't have to say anything else."

"Declan, please. I've not discussed any of this with another living soul. I feel like it's been sitting in me, rotting, and tearing me apart. I need to tell someone. Can't I tell you?"

Her offer of trust stunned him, and he nodded, determined not to sidetrack her heartfelt confession.

She took a deep breath. "We were a couple through my last two years of college and into the start of my career. He asked me to marry him shortly after my graduation but when asked about dates, his canned answer was 'Let's get some wings on my girl here and get her flying, then we'll talk about nesting.'"

Alexandria smiled, but it was bitter. He ached for her.

"I was thrilled that the love of my life was so supportive of getting my photography career off the ground. I didn't realize that his eyes were brown because he was full of shit."

Declan couldn't help the laugh that erupted and he nodded for her to continue.

"I had a wedding contract so I went to shoot the rehearsal photos and get the lay of the land for the wedding. But the ever-so-lovely couple had a knock-down-drag-out fight right at the start of the rehearsal and called everything off. I'd been really down after my mom died, so I went straight to Brent's apartment instead of meeting up with him later with our friends at Quencher's Saloon over on Western. I thought he could help me through, well, my misery."

Declan's gut tightened. An icy cold fist squeezed his heart. He wanted to stop her.

"I didn't think to knock, I just walked in, and I was so distracted that it wasn't until I was at the bedroom door that I realized he wasn't alone. He was with one of our "mutual" friends. I turned around and ran out."

Declan pulled her close. "I'm sorry. I'm sorry it happened, and I'm sorry I doubted that you knew how I felt. You didn't deserve that."

"Oh, I'm not done." Alexandria gave him a gentle hug and leaned back, her hands in her lap. "The worst is yet to come."

Declan felt clammy. He wasn't sure he wanted her to continue, but she seemed determined to finish purging herself.

"The ending of the relationship was tricky. I would have

liked nothing more than to knock his high-end veneers right off his teeth. I also knew that if either my dad or brother found out, they would go after him like rabid dogs. I couldn't let that happen. I knew there would be implications for Edin, both professionally and socially. My dad, too. The firm handles the bulk of his business and Brent's dad, Carl, is the founder and head partner. Carl could ruin Edin's career in a heartbeat and he is connected internationally like you wouldn't believe."

A warm and genuine smile transformed her face.

"Ever since I could remember, all Edin talked about being when he grew up was an attorney and the career he would have. I didn't want him to suffer because of my choices. I'd ignored Brent's calls, texts, and emails all weekend. I went to their office that Monday to find Brent. He was in Edin's office, discussing a deal over coffee. I knew from Edin's greeting that Brent hadn't said anything. I told him I needed a change, it was over, and gave him his ring. No reasons, no discussion. I packed my apartment, moved everything to Manitowoc, called my agent and booked an out-of-country job. I haven't really been back since."

Declan shook his head. "Damn."

Alexandria sighed. "I didn't think it would be a forever kind of exile, but Brent keeps stalking me, so the time kept extending. I thought he would get over it and move on. But he won't let it go and has insinuated on more than one occasion that he'll destroy Dad and Edin professionally if I don't come back. So, I just keep moving—only it keeps me away from everyone else."

"That explains a lot. Shit, Al, that sucks--but I don't see how that is the worst part."

"It's the worst part, because I told myself I acted to protect Edin and my dad and I truly believed I was. But this morning, when Edin and I were at the pool, I realized my cure was worse than the disease. Edin believed I'd gone off the deep end over Mom. He thought I was purposely avoiding him and Dad. I hurt them deeply."

Her head sagged forward and she pressed her eyes closed. Declan put his finger under her chin and pulled her up to face him. "You did what you thought was right. Now that you realize differently, you can change it. It's just a matter of choices. They love you and don't want to lose you again."

Determination lit her eyes and she smiled. "You're right. I've just been so isolated from them. I've lost my perspective. I've talked to no one. I feel like any slip of the tongue and Edin, or my dad, for that matter, would rip into Brent, and the shit storm would be on. What a dirt-bag, I can't believe I loved him once."

Declan gave a wry smile. "Gee, and I just thought he was an enormous asshole."

She tilted her head to the side and shot him an assessing look. "You always hire assholes as your attorneys?"

He laughed. "You might want to rethink that comment, since your brother is my attorney, not Brent. Never been impressed with that twerp."

"But your expedition letter came from Brent."

Declan shrugged. "I didn't...wait, is that why you refused?"

Twisting her hands in her lap, she nodded her head. "But now I have to see him and I don't know what to do. I won't give up my family again, but I don't want them harmed."

Wanting to give the right guidance, Declan paused. "Obviously, I'm probably not the best person to get relation-ship advice from..." As she outright laughed at him, Declan raised a brow. "However, Edin told me the lengths they went to in order to have you here."

He watched a flush of pink course over her cheeks and grabbed her hand, twining his fingers with hers. "Those aren't the actions of men who care more about their professional lives than the love they have for you. Trust them. It's Christmas, give them, and yourself, a gift. Live in the present."

Alexandria smiled. "You have pretty good advice for an old relationship slacker."

"Did you just call me old?" Declan couldn't believe his ears and was sure the shock showed on his face.

Alexandria squealed and jumped off the rock, grabbing her backpack. As she headed towards the coastal trail head, she tossed a seductive smile over her shoulder at him. "You could always prove me wrong, big fella."

Alexandria felt a million pounds lighter. She couldn't remember when she'd felt this happy, even with an obviously offended Declan following her down the cliff side trail. Maybe the "old" thing was a bit harsh, but hopefully, he would rise to the occasion and challenge her. Something had definitely risen to the occasion earlier when he kissed her. Despite the sweetness of his gentle kiss, she had felt the hardness of his erection pressed against her.

She didn't know if the depth of his desire was purely physical, but there seemed to be something more between them. Fantasy collided with reality. A handful of steps behind walked a gorgeous man who was confident, sexy, and successful, not to mention he'd earned the respect of both her father and brother. Unlike Brent, he didn't *need* her or her material resources. His touch set her on fire. She wanted someone who wanted her, not her connections or her inheritance. But as she reflected on his confession, the fire of fantasy cooled substantially. He had been hurt, too, and her intuition told her it went deeper than the casual explanation he'd provided.

On impulse, she stopped and whipped around.

Declan was heated, and not in the way he usually enjoyed. Surely, she didn't really believe he was *old*. She had challenged him to prove her wrong, and the animal in him was quick to accept a challenge. He loved a good competition, and all his instincts told him she would give him a run for his money. But if he succeeded, he would have to run with his money. His ties with Edin and John would be severed. He blew out a frustrated breath. Plus, Alexandria wasn't a prize. Her challenge was a tease. She'd finally gotten an enormous burden off her chest, and what a lovely chest it was, and now she was feeling...playful.

He glanced down the trail at her and smiled. He could play and play nice. After all, it was Christmas, and maybe some innocent fun was the best gift he could give her.

On the trail up, she had been informative but factual, but now, as she walked, she talked. Pointing out flora and fauna—he had to admit she had good eyes, not much got past her—she was a veritable Barbie tour guide.

This trail wound down the island, sometimes following the descending cliff line but other times winding through the jungle, past fragrant Frangipani, jasmine, coconut palms, and jack fruit trees. He was busy admiring a twenty-foot vine of scarlet passionfruit blooms when she turned and stopped in the trail, and he walked right into her. Her air left her in a whoof, and his arms went around her protectively. "What the hell! You need brake lights."

"Maybe you should watch me."

He let go.

She stepped back, a wide smile on her face.

Declan grabbed the front straps on his backpack to keep from pulling her to him. *Oh, baby, I have been watching you. If you only knew.*

"Declan, you're not old." She stepped a little closer and laid her hand flat on his chest, over his heart. He wondered if she noticed it missing some beats as her fingers softly moved. But then, all his blood was being pumped into his dick at the moment.

He cleared his throat. "I know."

"I was thinking, maybe we could be friends. I don't have many these days, and maybe we could discuss the Kukenam Tepui expedition." She looked him directly in the eye. "If Brent has no involvement with your firm and won't be involved in any manner or benefit from it, I will reconsider. If you still want me."

Declan smiled. This he could appreciate. "So as long as we can assure you Brent won't benefit in the slightest, you'll consider joining us?"

"A little vengeful or heartless?" Her teeth tugged her lip.

"Not at all. In my world, I consider it just desserts." His reassurances to her were realizations to him. He didn't want that spineless prick to benefit in any way, shape, or form from knowing her. The fact that he had once touched her made everything Neanderthal rise in him, and he wanted to pound Brent into a boneless mass of misery.

He smiled at her and ran his thumb along her jawline. "Friends it is. Partners in crime, if need be."

CHAPTER TEN

Edin stopped so fast that Meredith, Margaret, and John ran into his behind, knocking him one step farther into the great room. He couldn't have managed another step on his own. The beginning of rumbled complaints stopped abruptly. Edin rubbed his eyes in disbelief.

Meredith kindly put her index finger under his chin and shoved his jaw up to close his mouth.

None of which was even slightly noticed by the room's only occupants. The soundtrack from *Rudolph the Red-Nosed Reindeer* was blaring from the iPod dock, which wasn't so strange, as it was Alexandria's favorite Christmas video.

Nor was the fact that the gently domed ceiling of the great room was adorned with dozens and dozens of shiny Christmas balls, suspended from ribbons and mounted to the ceiling with thumbtacks. Green, red, gold, silver, blue, and purple caught the late afternoon light and shot sparkles of color throughout the room. Odd, maybe a little weird, but not strange.

What reeked of strangeness to Edin was Declan. He

stood tall in the middle of the room with Alexandria sitting on his shoulders as she stretched to mount more ornaments on the ceiling. *Did I not make myself clear? She is off limits!*

He must have made some noise, for Declan turned to face him.

Alexandria, sitting on Declan's shoulders with his arms gripping her calves for stability, held ornaments in each hand.

His sister was grinning like an imp.

"Hey guys, isn't this awesome? We couldn't find a ladder, so I drafted Declan into service. You guys won't let us help you, and we decided we needed more Christmas. Hey, what's for dinner tonight? Do you need any help?"

From the corner of his eye, Edin saw Margaret close Dad's mouth, and he burst into laughter. What. The. Hell. "Holy crap. Did you guys tour the island or stay here and pound Red Bull?"

Alexandria punched her last two ornaments into place with thumbtacks and started to dismount.

Declan helped her slide around and down his body like a Cirque du Soliel performer to land laughing by his side.

He shrugged at Edin with a look that said they would talk later. "We toured. Barbie took me."

"Barbie?"

"Yeah, didn't you know your sister is a veritable Barbie tour guide? She led me from one end of this island to the other. I saw the waterfall pool, the cliffs, two of the three full island trails, the lagoon, the tide pools, the tidal caves, the reef, the cottages, the harbor, the personal water-craft docks, every species of tree, flower, bird, lizard, and ..." he looked at Alexandria, "did I miss anything?"

She laughed. "The full house tour, including storage and warehouses."

"Yeah, those, too. I must have gotten the family special. I think the only thing I haven't seen, or heard about, is your dirty skivvies."

Alexandria smacked Declan in the arm and stuck her tongue out at him. Edin started in surprise at her playfulness. "So, what is all this?" He waved his hand to the ceiling.

Alexandria blushed. "I found the bulbs in storage and I thought we could hang them here, kinda like your own disco ballroom." She raised one brow at Edin. "Unless, of course, you've already got one?"

Meredith laughed. "I knew I forgot something!"

John and Margaret ducked past them with smiles, heading for the kitchen.

Declan swallowed his very fine merlot and realized that, other than the hard on in his pants, he was having a blast. The remembered scent of Alexandria's skin was fresh in his mind and the feel of her sitting on his shoulders, the smooth creamy length of her thighs so close to his mouth made him hungry for something other than the succulent prime rib sitting on his plate.

Listening to John regale Meredith with the story of Edin's first camping trip, Declan tried to focus. He had forgotten over the years what it was like to be part of a family; the incessant banter rolling around him reminded him of dinners with his cousins. But his family had not been like this; this family pulled you in and made you part of them.

There had always just seemed to be so many cousins, and they had all grown up close to each other. His three aunts spent most of their time together and so had their kids. As an only child destined to take over for his father, he had always felt set apart, like he didn't belong. But where did he belong?

Alexandria was eating like she hadn't in a week. As she slathered butter on a hot roll, she turned her attention to Edin. "When do the first guests arrive? Or do they all show at once?"

"Rudy, Leann, and Brent arrive tomorrow. The Greenleys, Victor, and *Lucy*?" he quirked an eyebrow in question at Meredith, "Arrive on Thursday."

"I guess that's her name. She was a last minute add." Meredith merely shrugged. "They can't be all that serious, since they are set up for separate rooms, and we still haven't met her."

"I can go to Saipan for pick up," Declan offered to Edin.

"Thanks, but Mere has a couple of appointments and I have some business to finish."

"If you guys are game, we could go snorkeling tomorrow before we have to leave?" Meredith took up the reins.

"I'm in," Alexandria said as she moved to catch a drip of butter on her tongue.

As Declan imagined her warm pink tongue in other places, his dick tightened painfully.

"I'm assuming I'm the wedding photographer, so we could also discuss what you'd like."

"Well, yes and no, baby girl," John said.

Her wide-eyed gaze flew to her father.

He smiled. "Yes, they want you to be the photographer, but you're in the wedding, too, so you'll need some help."

Declan wanted to laugh when she smiled in a cat-that-ate-the-canary way.

"I've already planned for that."

John looked taken aback. "I do my job as well as you do

yours, Dad." She turned to Edin. "When you go to Saipan Thursday, a guy named Tim Martinez from J.L. Baker & Sons will be looking for you. I gave him your cell number and your time window. He'll have some crates for you. I'll need those."

John, Margaret, and Meredith stared at her, but Edin just smiled.

Declan took the bait. "Who is Tim and what will he have?"

Her smile was radiant. "Christmas Eve, I realized the logistics of being in a wedding and getting photos shot. I'd planned to leave from here in January for a short shoot with Nat Geo in Costa Rica, so my remote gear was crated and ready to go. But since I'll need it here, I texted my agent and had him air freight it out on Christmas Eve. Since we're a day ahead of them, it all worked perfectly. Well, sort of. He was a little late to dinner, and his wife was pissed, but she can just get over it. For what I pay him, she can deal with him being ten minutes late. Anyway, it will be here Thursday, so all I need to know is how many, what kind of shots you'd really like, and to plan the "pre-event" photo layouts."

Edin didn't seem the least bit surprised with her planning.

Looking at her, John's chest puffed and he sat up a little taller. "Well, aren't you a chip off the old block."

Declan was impressed himself. She had acted fast to plan for what just barely registered with him. No wonder Al Marsh was regarded as a kick ass, take-no-prisoners professional.

Declan pulled himself up onto the jetty and water sluiced

off his body. He shook his head and droplets flew everywhere.

As the warm salty spray hit him, Edin snapped. "Hey! Do you have to shake like a damn dog?"

Declan flopped down beside his friend, hanging his long legs into the water. Leaning back, he braced his hands on the sun-warmed wood.

"Get to it, Edin. What's on your mind?"

"Did I or did I not tell you to stay the hell away from her?" Edin ground out.

Declan sat upright and looked him in the eye. "Yes, you did..."

"So, what part of that fucking conversation did you not get?" Edin jerked his head toward Alexandria and Meredith, who were snorkeling near the shallow reef which circled the island.

Declan's jaw clenched, but he tried to remember Edin's words were born of worry for Alexandria. "I didn't miss any part of it. She and I have come to an...an agreement." He would have laughed at the look on Edin's face, but he liked his teeth right where they were.

"An *agreement*? What the fuck are you doing?"

Declan felt the sharp bite of the double-edge blade. *Damned if I do, damned if I don't.* What had he gotten himself into? Edin was his friend—a true one. His mind raced over his early morning conspiracy with Al. He sighed. "I agreed to a deal with her."

"A deal?"

He snapped a little. "Yeah, a fuckin' deal. You might recognize what those are, right? It's simple. You invited her ex-fiancé to your wedding. She wants a little male company for the week as a buffer."

"She asked you for this? How hard did you try to talk her out of it?"

"I didn't."

"I bet not. What are you getting out of it?"

"She'll reconsider the expedition."

Declan continued, cutting off Edin's possible retort. "It may not mean much, but I told her you and John don't find me acceptable for her and wouldn't like the idea."

Edin ducked his head and glanced away. "You told her that?"

"Yeah, but she didn't seem impressed." He looked hard at Edin's profile, saw the conflict in his friend, and drove his point home. "This is your fault, you know. If Brent wasn't coming, she wouldn't be cutting deals. I understand why you did, though."

Edin's shoulders sagged, and he looked back at Declan. "What exactly do you think you understand?"

"If you can get her through dealing with Brent, she'll have no excuses for avoiding Chicago and your nicely packaged family unit." Declan rose to his feet and looked down at Edin. "What really sucks is that neither of you actually trust her judgment. She's fucking amazing, and I'm not talking about her looks." He turned and stalked off the jetty, heading across the beach back toward the housing compound.

Meredith pushed her mask and snorkel up to perch on her head, one foot pressing lightly on a rock between the sections of the hard-coral reef while her arms swayed back and forth, keeping her vertical in the warm, buoyant tropical waters. From the corner of her eye, she could see bright tropical fish flitter through the crystal-clear water, but her focus was on the woman before her.

Meredith watched Alexandria's gaze move from Declan's retreating figure to her brother. She smiled at the look of frustration on Al's face. Edin got that same look when he was pondering some massive issue, and she marveled that she felt such an attachment to her soon-to-be sister-in-law when, for most of her life, she'd avoided close friendships.

"So—you and Declan?"

Alexandria jerked and turned to face her. "What?"

"You and Declan. Seems you're hitting it off right nicely."

She watched Alexandria tread water, physically and mentally. Her years in the medical field had taught her that sometimes people needed a bit of silence to process their thoughts, and it appeared Alexandria's were churning vats of butter.

Meredith glanced at the jetty, where Edin stared at the open ocean, deep in thought. She decided to take matters in hand. "Come on." She swam toward the large rocks of the lagoon area across from the quay.

She didn't need Edin interrupting her. To her surprise, Alexandria followed obediently and without comment, which only indicated a lot of activity thrashed around inside that pretty head.

Scaling the rocks Alexandria perched next to Meredith on the outcropping. She was looking at Edin again. Meredith touched Alexandria's hand to get her attention. "Just because he's my fiancé doesn't mean I tell him everything or that we agree on everything."

Alexandria smiled but didn't respond, so Meredith

forged ahead. "Edin and your dad have been very anxious to see you."

Alexandria opened her mouth, but Meredith held her hand up. "Please don't. I would like to give you my point of view."

Alexandria nodded. "Okay."

"First and foremost, I think you're amazing and I'm thrilled we'll be related. However, that doesn't mean we're always going to agree." She watched Alexandria carefully. "I would have to be daft not to see the attraction between you and Declan."

Alexandria's eyes widened. "That being said, I'm pretty sure he is also not someone with whom your dad and brother would want you to have a relationship. He has a reputation as a ladies man."

"Yeah, I've heard that." Alexandria got her first words in.

"Really? From whom?"

"Declan told me. He said he was told to stay away from me."

It was Meredith's turn to be surprised. "Really? Dec told you?"

"Yes, but I don't really see how it is anyone's damn business—"

"You're right. It isn't anyone's business but yours, and you strike me as being pretty darn savvy and able to hold your own."

"Really? I'm getting the impression everyone thinks I'm an idiot basket case who requires constant manipulation."

Angst supercharged every word. "Well, I don't. Nor do I agree with Edin and Dad. I don't think Margaret does, either."

"Which part? That I'm a basket case or that I need to be handled?"

"Neither. I'm of the opinion that Declan has been hurt, and he uses his rep as a defense."

"I thought you were a nurse, not a shrink."

"It's your business, but I think he's a good guy, and you look great together. Don't let anyone make your mind up for you."

Edin was swimming toward them so Meredith pushed off the rock back into the warm, salty sea. She turned to smile at Alexandria. "So, should we invent an absentee fiancé before Brent arrives? Or go with the hot guy on hand?"

CHAPTER ELEVEN

Declan scrubbed the shampoo through his hair with more ferocity than was probably wise. His scalp felt like he was taking the skin off, but the ache couldn't distract him from thoughts of the green eyes that seemed to haunt his every waking moment. He rinsed his hair and leaned against the shower wall, letting the hot water pound against him. *What the hell is wrong with me?*

He couldn't get Alexandria out of his thoughts. If she wasn't physically in his face, he was thinking of her and wondering where she was like some lovesick dumb shit. To make matters worse, he had complicated the situation by agreeing to be the guy of the week, putting himself in the crosshairs of both Edin and John.

He shut the water off and grabbed a towel from the stack on the shelf, wrapping it around his waist. Snatching a second towel, he padded from the bathroom across the thick carpet to stand in front of the tall windows facing the sea vista. His room was at the end of the guest wing, farthest from the main great room building, affording him a measure of solitude and privacy. The elevation of the compound and the design of the buildings allowed for broad views of the Pacific Ocean while the jungle, sloping sharply away from right to left provided a view of the far side of the pool deck where the trails to points everywhere originated.

The late afternoon sunlight danced over the water, soothing him. A glance at the clock on the bedside table confirmed that Edin should soon be back from Saipan with Rudy, Leann, and Brent.

A flash of movement caught his attention. The object of his frustrations crossed the pool deck to the trail that led down to the beach. Sun-kissed skin was set off by the white summer dress and sandals that graced her statuesque figure. Her hair was down, and he realized he hadn't seen it down and loose since the day he met her. Now, like then, he wanted to lose himself in the soft curls. Suddenly, he realized he had also never seen her in a dress. *Shit, she's preparing for battle.*

He finished drying off and dressed in record time, combed his hands back through his hair as he jetted through the door and headed to the trail. He'd be lucky to catch her before she reached the dock area, and he had a few things he wanted to confirm with her before this charade went any further. He would back her play, but there had to be some rules—for her protection as well as his own.

As Alexandria stepped from the trail onto the golf cart path to the busy docks, she took a deep breath. Maybe she should have asked Declan to come with her, but she wasn't sure she could handle him and Brent in the same moment. Whenever Dec was close, she felt like was spun about in circles and shot out of a cannon. Every fiber in her being came to life.

She was uncertain enough about this initial reunion with Brent. She didn't have a clue what direction his greeting would take, and she needed her wits in one place. Not scattered on the winds of her attraction to Declan.

Ahead of her, Edin and Rudy were tying the boat up while Rudy's wife, Leann, watched. Rudy had grown up down the street and, together with Edin, had tormented her from early childhood with their boyish pranks.

How the bold and outgoing Rudy had snagged the heart of the quiet and reserved Leann was a mystery to her. But then, she had missed more than she cared to think about in the last four years.

A second boat was tied up to the other dock, and several workers were preparing to unload the two boats.

Brent stood surveying the activity around him. Walking closer her smile faded. He seemed shorter than she remembered, just a little taller than her own five-foot-eleven, lean and trim from his years of tennis. His tan Diesel shorts and pastel Tommy Bahama, button-up shirt accentuated his pale, midwestern winter skin. She somehow remembered him as tanner than this. But he was still handsome. His brush-cut, black-brown hair was all business, and his dark brown eyes were hidden behind Bentley shades. She couldn't decide if he was more GQ or Maxim.

When he saw her he headed for her at a sharp clip. She moved forward to ensure they met in the midst of all the people bustling about, stopping face to face where the sand met the boardwalk.

She glanced over his shoulder and saw Edin tossing commands to dock hands before he also headed her way. "Hello Brent," she said, looking Brent in the eye.

"Hey, there, Alley Cat. You look fabulous."

His long, lingering appraisal made her skin crawl.

"I didn't like the nickname Alley Cat four years ago. What makes you think I would like it any more now?" She pressed her lips together, and her eyes narrowed.

Brent smiled and ran his hand from her shoulder to her elbow.

She trembled and barely refrained from slapping his hand away.

He shrugged. "Sorry, it just slipped out. I've missed you. You don't return my emails or calls."

Alexandria stepped back but collided with a hard body. Declan's warm earthy scent enfolded her, even as his arms settled around her waist.

"Hey, baby, sorry I'm late." He left his arm around her waist as he planted himself firmly at her side. He offered his right hand to Brent. "Hey, Brent, Happy Holidays."

Edin came up beside Brent, his inquiring gaze turned to Declan, close by Alexandria. He held Declan's gaze, and the slight incline of his head blessed the deception.

Brent's cocky grin died as he looked from Declan to Alexandria. He shook the proffered hand stiffly. "Thanks, same to you, Declan. I didn't know you'd be here."

Alexandria glanced up at Declan, who smiled lazily and stroked her back. "We arrived on Christmas Eve."

As Brent stiffened beside him, Edin bit back a grin.

Rudy and Leann joined the group, and Alexandria slipped from Declan's side to greet them. Rudy was her height, but his thick, muscular build made her feel small in his firm hug. Rudy was closest thing she had to another brother. His affectionate greeting played discordant notes on her already strained heartstrings. Between his ginger hair and beard, and ruddy complexion, the only link missing to his Scottish ancestors was a kilt. She admired Rudy. He lived by his family motto of "Fac et Spera." "Do and hope" definitely fit his personality.

She turned from Rudy's arms to Leann. Despite being petite to the point Alexandria had to bend more than a little to hug her, she felt no fragility in Leann's fierce hug. Her stick-straight, honey blonde hair was swept up, but a few loose tendrils blew in the breeze and tickled Alexandria's face. Her fawn brown eyes brimmed with happiness. Leann was possessed of an artless beauty that reminded Alexandria of the *Mona Lisa*.She had always wanted to photograph her. Leann was all things soft and gentle, and Alexandria wondered once again at the magic between the lion and the lamb.

CHAPTER TWELVE

Alexandria shot bolt upright in her bed, her gaze darting around the darkened room. Moonlight filtering through the patchy cloud cover did little to illuminate the lurking shadows. Her thundering heart would not still, and an overwhelming sense of loss fell over her. She rose from the bed and went to the windows. Pressing her forehead to the smooth glass, she focused on breathing in a long, determined rhythm to slow her heart rate. As she did so, glimpses of her dream rose to her conscious state.

She stood in the velvety darkness. She could feel him, a rock-hard body pressed to the length of her. The heat of his chest warmed the muscles of her back and she relaxed into him. His hand swept her hair up and off her neck. The cool feel of air replaced by the warmth of lips pressed to the tender skin at the base of her hairline. His other hand glided over her hip and around the bottom of her rib cage, lightly caressing ever closer to her aching breasts. They felt heavy and full with yearning. His lips traced a warm trail behind her ear and down the side of her throat to the curve of her neck. Her collarbone. Heat and desire pulsed through her.

She wanted more. The edge of his left thumb teased the underside of her breast while his splayed fingers moved lightly over her ribs and abdomen. His right hand combed through her hair, massaging her scalp, and she felt the flow of her hair's movement under his hand like a second silky caress. Her thighs warmed and molten heat coiled low inside her. She craved to feel him there. He turned her in his arms and her tender breasts skimmed his chest making her nipples tighten with need. As she parted her lips in anticipation of his kiss, incoherent murmurs of need escaped her. But his heat and strength pulled away. His hand slid down her shoulder, caressed her elbow, her forearm, until his palm cupped the back of her hand. He turned his face into her palm, cupping his cheek with her hand. She marveled at the strong line of the clean-shaven jaw. The power beneath her fingers. His warm breath tickled her inner wrist, his fingers teased her knuckles. Turning his face, he pressed his lips to the palm of her hand. Lightning raced up her arm, and her head fell back. His tongue followed the kiss, licking the tender lines of her palm. And then, he was gone.

Alexandria's cheeks warmed and she slid her hand to cup her breast. It was full and achy and sensitive, just like the juncture of her thighs. A deep breath in, a long slow release of air, and she shook herself. This was ridiculous. The pitch black of her dream could not hide the identity of her lover. The dreamed scents and the touches, the curve of his jaw...Declan.

CHAPTER THIRTEEN

The rough granite rock was warm beneath her butt, and the mid-day sun beat down on her. Alexandria leaned back, bracing her hands flat on the large stone, and lifted her face to the sun, her eyes closed behind her Vuarnet sunglasses. The soft breeze touched her face like gentle fingers, gliding over and around her, pulling at errant wisps of her hair. She smiled and burrowed her feet into the warm, wet sand. The sea was gentle today, the push and tug of the waves on her feet and calves a soothing balm. The warmth and peace of it chased away all conscious thought, and she gave herself over to just feeling. Relaxation washed over her, and her mind wandered where it would.

A shadow crossed over the sun. Her skin shivered and Alexandria sat up sharply, shadowing her eyes with one hand. "What are you doing here?"

Brent stepped closer. "I wanted to talk to you, but you've been avoiding me since I arrived."

"Figured that out all by yourself, did you?" Alexandria got to her feet and stood firm.

"You never gave me a chance to explain."

"Your actions were quite clear. You don't need to explain anything."

"I do. I loved you. I still do, and you just threw it all away."

Alexandria snorted. "*I* threw it away?" She stared Brent straight in the eye. "It was pretty clear when you were balls deep in your little heiress that you were right where you wanted to be." She took a step closer. "I ended it as painlessly as possible for everyone. My brother would have mounted your head on a pike and my dad would have disposed of the body—consider yourself lucky."

She turned to walk away.

Brent grabbed her arm and spun her back to face him. "Wait, Al, there's so much you don't know."

Alexandria jerked her arm out of his grasp. "I can't think of anything I need to know."

"Oh, really? Like where were you all those nights when it could have been us in each other's arms?" Brent strode a few steps away and turned back, jabbing his finger in her face. "Where were you when I needed you? All ice princess and wanting to wait for the wedding. I needed a woman, not a little girl. I tried to wait for you to grow up, but you just kept pushing me away. I was lonely and I made a mistake. I've been paying for it ever since."

Alexandria stared at Brent, mouth gaping. He apparently took her silence as a good sign and reached for her right hand, pulling it close.

He watched his thumb caress her palm. "Al, baby, I've missed you so much. She didn't mean anything to me. I only love you. She was just a way to release my tensions so I could be there for you, the way you wanted me to be."

Alexandria grabbed his pinky finger with her left hand and yanked it backwards.

The pain straightened Brent upright, and he released her hand.

The surprise and pain in his eyes barely had time to register before her right fist smashed into his face. His ass hit the wet sand. "Brent, I am many things, but stupid is not on the list. No honorable person fucks someone else and spouts such stupid bullshit for an excuse. Your shit ends here, today. I never told my family what happened because I didn't see the point of dragging that shit out of the closet. But if you don't stay the hell away from me, I'll hand you your ass myself. I've grown up. I don't need my family to do it for me. So, Brent, fuck off." She turned and stalked off the beach, grabbing her sandals as she went.

From his vantage point behind the thickly vined trees, Declan saw and heard the scene play out before him. He was close enough to intervene if anything went awry, but he knew that Alexandria would not welcome his interference now. He'd followed Brent with every intention of telling him to stay the hell away from Alexandria, but he hadn't caught him before Brent made it to the open beach and the lovely red-haired spitfire. When she gave her former fiancé a super-sized knuckle sandwich, he nearly laughed out loud. Declan grinned. You didn't find a girl like that just anywhere. He watched as she strode off the beach like an Amazon warrior and onto the trail leading to the main house.

He turned his attention back to Brent, who was just getting back on his feet, staring after Alexandria.

"Oh, you'll be mine again, you little bitch," Brent

sneered, "and this time, I won't be so considerate of your feelings."

As Brent stomped away, his words carried to Declan clearly on the warm breeze. Rage coiled in Declan and he stepped forward, fully intending to go after the worthless bastard.

"Practicing our voyeur skills, are we?" Rudy's slight brogue sliced quietly through his murderous thoughts.

Declan's sharp retort was cut short as Rudy continued. "I think we should follow the little prick and feed him his own for good measure, but I'm not sure how we'll be explaining that to the family and keeping the lass's secret."

"You heard?"

Rudy nodded his head. "Oh yeah. I was coming 'round the other side when I heard them start in, and when I tried to go around, I saw you. Awful busy little section of the jungle, if you ask me."

Declan clenched his teeth and stared at Rudy. He didn't know this guy from Adam and wasn't sure what to make of him.

Rudy shrugged. "I'd offer to buy you a shot, but all I actually have to do is pour it. What do you say? We can toast a lovely lass with a damned nice right hook and her secrets."

Declan nodded slowly. "And the little prick?"

Rudy looked at him, measuring him. "I do believe revenge is best served cold."

His regard for Rudy increased exponentially. A grim smile slowly spread on Declan's face. He nodded. "I usually go for hot and fast. But in this case, I think cold and hard will do. Let's get a drink."

CHAPTER FOURTEEN

John dropped his sunglasses on the counter and looked through the great room to the pool deck. His island seemed a little crowded. Alexandria, Declan, Rudy, Meredith, and Leann were sprawled over chairs and lounges by the bar, chatting. Edin would be back any minute with the remaining guests, and the next few days promised to be a flurry of activity. Originally, this had seemed like a good idea, but he was having his doubts.

Margaret's arms slid around her husband's waist and held him close. "You seem lost in thought."

"Yeah."

"Time to share, darling."

John sighed. "I thought this would be a good way to get Al back, show her how we missed her, and get her to live in the present."

"And it's not?"

When Brent walked up to join the group, Declan moved close to Alexandria's side. John's eyes narrowed. "I don't like how cozy she is with Declan."

Margaret pressed close and moved to his side. She

watched the group on the patio for a moment before turning her attention to John. "Honey, you see Alexandria as she was four years ago."

"What?"

"Four years ago, impacted by loss, breaking up with Brent, and disappearing. You don't seem to be able to see her as she is now. As much as you want her to live in the present, you need to do so, also."

As he looked at his wife, tenderness filled him. "I'm not sure what to do."

"Maybe you don't have to do anything but respect her choices and let her make them."

"What if she chooses to disappear again? Or gets involved with Declan?"

"If she does, it will be her choice, and you'll have to deal with that when it happens. Your constant angst isn't helping." She looked at the group by the pool. "But I don't think she will."

"Will what? Disappear or get hurt?"

"Either." Margaret smiled. "I have it on good authority she cut a deal with Declan to stay close and pretend to be her guy in return for reconsidering his expedition."

"Why would she do that?" he asked.

"Why indeed? Why would she be setting up a fake boyfriend? Maybe that is the question that begs an answer." She kissed his cheek and swept into the kitchen.

John stared after her momentarily and turned to watch his daughter, deep in thought.

CHAPTER FIFTEEN

As they made their way down the hall for dinner, Alexandria and Declan laughed and chatted. She felt tingles at the base of her spine where his hand rested. He conducted her through the doorway, relating a funny mishap from one of his many expeditions.

When he stopped abruptly and went silent, she looked at him. Cold, hard, angry eyes stared across the great room. A tic in his cheek and palpable tension made him a implacable stranger. She glanced across the room to the object of his intense focus. A voluptuous platinum blonde with an airbrushed tan perched on a stool at the bar. The room seemed crowded with all of Edin's guests in close proximity and the only one Alexandria didn't know was the blonde.

The woman's gaze went to Declan, and a sultry smile grew just for him. Comprehension hit Al like a ton of bricks, and she wanted to rip the bitch's heart out. Stunned by her strong reaction, Alexandria's grip tightened on Declan's arm. He turned to her.

She tried to convey her support and understanding with

her eyes and the unrelenting grip on his arm. When he relaxed and put his arm around her shoulder, she knew he got her message.

From the corner of her eye, she saw the blonde's smile waver. She leaned close. "Looks like the terms have changed and now I've got your back," she whispered.

Declan put his hand on the small of Alexandria's back and guided her forward. Greetings were flying and they paused to say hello as they worked their way across the room to where Edin stood with his latest group of guests. Tom, Rosamund, and Victor greeted Alexandria without pause, while Edin introduced Declan.

Victor moved to stand beside the blonde. He smiled blandly. "This is—"

"Louisa," Declan said.

The group stilled at his tone.

Hesitating, Edin glanced between them and then to Alexandria.

Louisa laughed. "Oh, Declan, no need to be so formal and stiff. I've gotten used to the nickname Lucy, although I'm sure I'll always be Louisa to you."

"I take it you two know each other?" Edin butted in.

Declan glanced at Alexandria, recognizing the concern in her eyes, and back to Edin. "We ran in the same circles once upon a time," he said, "but I can't say we truly knew each other." His hand caressed Alexandria's back. Awkward silence hung heavy in the air.

"Well, at least we know everyone knows someone." Meredith's perky voice snapped everyone back into action. "It seems dinner is ready, and Margaret's outdone herself."

The glass wall of the great room was folded back to welcome the evening breezes. Candle lanterns on the pool deck perfumed the air with citronella. Guests and family were settled on sofas, love seats, armchairs, and chaise lounges. Glasses of wine and cold beer added their heady scents to the night, and conversation flowed.

Tension coiled in Alexandria's chest and her stomach churned. Neither she nor Declan had much appetite during the meal, and the post-dinner chatter about wedding plans and pre-nuptial events wasn't doing much to alleviate her anxiety.

With only five days left until Edin's wedding, the social calendar he and Meredith had briefly outlined was busier than a commercial tour guide's. Declan never strayed from her side during the evening, keeping himself between her and Brent like a shield. She wasn't sure if his mood was darker when he contemplated Brent or when his glance moved to Louisa. She shifted closer to Declan on the love-seat and breathed in his warm, earthy scent that made her think of starlit skies and growing things.

On the adjacent love-seat, Tom and Rosamund relaxed.

Alexandria had photographed their wedding five years ago. The soft, loving glow that resonated in their wedding photos still radiated between them. She squelched her pangs of envy, a stark reminder of how she had felt at their wedding.

A software security engineer, Tom was tall, lean, and quiet. Reputed to be brilliant at his job, very little escaped him in day-to-day life, either. Soft-spoken almost to a fault, he preferred the buzz of computers to the company of most people. He didn't speak much, but when he did, people usually listened. His bright green-eyed gaze scanned the room before returning to Rosamund.

With a gentle smile, Rosamund brushed back a lock of his light brown hair that was nearly the exact same shade as her own shoulder-length, wavy layered cut. While privacy and security were Tom's watchwords, they weren't Rosamund's, which put Alexandria on alert when Rosamund turned to her. Snuggling into the curve of Tom's arm, her pixie face was avid with curiosity, brown eyes glowing.

"Last year, I saw your photos in that conservancy magazine about the snow leopards. They were amazing."

Alexandria felt the attention of the room. "Thank you."

"How long did it take to get those photos?" Rosamund inquired.

"Yeah, how does it all work?" Leann chimed in.

Her heart started to hammer at the thought of being at the center of a storm of questions, but Declan's arm moved behind her on the sofa, his fingers barely grazing the skin of her shoulder. Something akin to an electric sedative flowed through her, slowing her pulse and calming her heartbeat. "We spent six months working with the local conservancy agents who had been tracking sightings. Most of the photos were taken in the Lake Baikal area in southern Siberia and the Kunlun Mountains along the northern Tibetan plateau."

"Six months?" Leann blurted. "Do you travel in an RV?"

"No." Alexandria smiled. "We traveled mostly by Humvee and Arctic Trucks. Kunlun has only two highways and neither went where we needed to go, so it was all off-road." To Alexandria's dismay, everyone seemed utterly and completely fascinated by the photo hunt for big cats.

Margaret paused in her embroidery. "But how do you find the leopards?"

"We set up base camp far enough away not to impact the wildlife. You can't take vehicles into the observation areas because they drive everything away, so we'd backpack in."

"Backpack?" Meredith's face scrunched up. "And then what?"

"You carry in what you need, but minimal. You can't be setting up another campsite. I don't like the guides carrying my equipment, so I tote my own stuff."

"So, you hike around looking for snow leopards?"

Despite being on a tropical island in the middle of the Pacific Ocean, Meredith seemed at a total loss for anything remotely related to being in the wild. Alexandria shook her head slightly. "No. You locate a prime position, downwind from the sighting areas, you set up your blind, and you wait —sometimes for days."

"Skip the hiking part. Think of all the times you'd be pooing in the woods!" Rudy laughed at the look on Meredith's face. "When you have to go, you have to go."

Alexandria ignored Rudy. "The whole purpose is to capture them in their world so we can help humans understand the impact we have on them and change that for the better." She half-shrugged. "They're not going to come to me."

"Isn't that why we have zoos?" Louisa's sultry voice interjected. Her smile didn't quite reach her eyes. "Captive, contained, at your mercy. All that."

"That defeats the purpose." Alexandria studied Louisa as she contemplated her response. The slightest hint of dark roots gave way to platinum waves that framed her heart-shaped face. Blue eyes with artfully applied soft, rosy shadows and liners accented her baby-doll sensuality. Full pink lips pouted in a face with porcelain smooth skin. Probably no taller than five-foot-five, she had a top-heavy hourglass figure and her clingy cornflower blue dress showed every curve to her advantage.

A momentary feeling of utter inadequacy threatened Alexandria's composure, but the slide of Declan's thumb across her bicep grounded her. "Humans, as well as environmental factors, have impacted wildlife beyond the normal person's perception. Recent estimates indicate only between four and six thousand snow leopards are left in the world, and they are just one of many endangered big cat species. No confirmed sightings of any South China tigers have been documented since the 1970's. Humans have a greater impact on the global environment than any other species on the planet. That should carry a responsibility to protect the planet and the life on it."

"Well said." Tom toasted her with his beer bottle. "Your work brings meaning and beauty to those of us without the resources to see it ourselves."

Rudy raised his beer, as well. "Hear, hear! I know Leann nearly emptied the savings account to support big cat preservation after that article."

That the friends she had left behind supported her efforts suffused her with pleasure--and a longing to once again enjoy the warmth of longtime friends. Across the way, Louisa watched her like a snake with a mouse.

"Al, I've got a couple of things I wanted to go over with you. I thought we could grab a few minutes in my room. Would you mind?"

Meredith's voice cut through her thoughts. "No, that would be fine." Alexandria rose to go with Meredith but turned to whisper in Declan's ear, "I'll be back as fast as I can. Don't kill anyone."

An honest laugh erupted, and he put his hand behind

her neck and pulled her close, kissing her lightly on the mouth. "I'll try not to. Just hurry back."

Frissons of pleasure flustered her. Meredith's hand on her arm moved her along.

"Well, if the lass doesna have the good sense to choose a Scot, at least she chose you, Ruaidhrí." Rudy's deep voice carried down the hall.

Alexandria smiled in spite of herself.

CHAPTER SIXTEEN

The door barely closed behind Alexandria when she found her arms full of a weeping Meredith.

"Oh my God. Al! I'm so sorry. I've messed everything up."

Startled and confused, Alexandria awkwardly comforted Meredith, patting her back and smoothing her hair. "I'm sorry, Mere, but I don't understand. What's messed up?"

Mere pulled back and stared at her. "For you and Declan. Brent is here making you feel awkward, and that horrid woman is leering all over at Declan. I don't know how they know each other, but it can't be good. You two were just starting to really connect."

"Mere, listen to me. It's going to be fine." Alexandria pushed her inner trepidations down. A girl only gets married once, at least that was the way it was supposed to be, and a diamond-hard determination was born in Al in that moment. Her hands cupped Meredith's face and turned her teary eyes up to face her. "You're going to be my sister and you will have a fabulous wedding here in paradise that you'll tell your grandkids about someday. I'll grant you that Brent is a useless douche, but I've already punched his lights out once today, and I have no issues over doing it again if need be. I can handle the plastic platinum bitch, too."

A feeble smile wobbled on Meredith's lips. "You punched him?"

Alexandria nodded, and they both broke into laughter. "Yeah, it was a right hook my dad would've been proud of."

Laughing, Meredith pulled Alexandria to the couch by the windows where she collapsed. Suddenly, she sat up and stared at Alexandria.

"But, why, why would you punch him? Unless..."

Alexandria sobered, her lips ready with a lie and then stopped. "Well, I could lie to you, but that doesn't feel right, I hate to lie."

"So don't."

"I broke the engagement because I caught him screwing around."

"So, why did you leave? Were you so broken hearted that you couldn't face anyone? You just took off and stayed away?"

Her mouth opened, but the words didn't come. She closed her mouth and looked at Meredith, who stared, waiting. She started again, slowly, measuring her words. "No. It's funny. Well, not funny like ha-ha, but funny like, like terribly messed up. In all this time, it never occurred to me that although I was hurt and angry and pissed beyond belief, I was never broken-hearted that the man I loved, or thought I loved, and was ready to spend my life with, was screwing someone else. My biggest and main concern was the damage he threatened to my family."

"What?"

"Brent's dad is one of the biggest movers and shakers in the Mid-West. Their law firm is in the top ten of the largest in the country and has international reach. Edin was just starting his career at the firm. Most of my dad's legal needs were handled by their firm. All I could think of was that if they got wind of Brent's fuck-up, literally, that one of them would lay into him and Brent's dad would initiate a vendetta that would ruin Edin's career or cause problems for my dad's businesses. Brent said if there were any issues, he'd make them pay."

Meredith gasped. "My God, Al, you have to tell them. They think you're mental over your mom. No offense."

Alexandria grabbed Meredith by the shoulders, ready to shake her. "No! You have to promise me you won't say anything."

"But this doesn't make sense."

"I know, but it doesn't have to anymore. My business with Brent is finished. When I saw him here, I realized that what I felt for him was, I don't know, but it wasn't love. Fascination, maybe? The naïve excitement that a guy as rich and attractive as him was interested in me, especially considering how freaky and ungainly I was."

Meredith worked her jaw a couple of times. "Excuse me?"

Alexandria smiled mischievously and swept both hands up and down to indicate her person. "Yeah, baby, hard to believe, but all this and a bag chips I wasn't always."

Meredith laughed. "Yeah, right."

"No, really, think about it. I was five-foot-ten in ninth grade with no sign of boobs. I was a freakin' giraffe. Wild red hair like one of those crazy-ass troll dolls, tomboy, top-of-the-class geek grades with a camera in my hand twenty-four-seven. Hard as it is to believe, the high school boys weren't quite lining up for that. I had to go to my senior prom with Edin, for cryin' out loud. My dad took me to the winter formal but refused prom because my classmates were hitting on him."

Meredith was laughing so hard tears were running down her cheeks. "I just can't picture that."

"Yeah, well, I'm know some photographic evidence is somewhere around here."

Meredith sobered. "So, what happened?"

Alexandria smiled. "I grew up. In college, the tomboy in me calmed down a little, and I grew some boobs. I hung out more with Edin and his friends. I met Brent and...I don't know, it just took on a life of its own. Maybe I thought that was what I was supposed to do or be."

"And now?"

"Now? Well, I have an amazing life. I travel. I earn my living doing the things I absolutely love and adore." Words and thoughts held deep inside for so long burst forth like a cleansing confessional. "And—and I can capture them so other people can share in some small way the miraculous and amazing things I am so blessed to experience. Oh God, Mere, I love my family so much, and I don't want to be alienated from them, but I would be so stifled to be in one place, doing the same thing all the time. I would suffocate. As much as I love them, as much as I wanted to protect them from harm, I think I wasn't as much running away from consequences in Chicago as I was running to find myself. To once and for all finally settle into my own skin, my own life, and to know who I am."

Meredith sidled close and held her hand. "So, who are you?"

"I'm Al, and I'm whatever I want to be."

"And where does Declan fit in that plan?"

CHAPTER SEVENTEEN

Several heavy-duty, Pelican storm cases littered the pool deck. Some lay open with various tools of Alexandria's trade peeking out of their protective beds. Standing by the table, an open case in front of her, Alexandria pulled first one lens then another from their foam cases. Popping the lens covers off and wiping their fragile glass eyes that framed her world with a soft cloth, her thoughts strayed far afield from the task at hand.

As visions of Declan filled her thoughts, her blood warmed. The innocent "deal" was disappearing under an avalanche of desire. His presence in her dreams ensured he was a constant companion. She couldn't reconcile his reputation to the man who stood guard for her peace of mind each day.

Not to mention, peace of mind was nowhere to be found when his warm, woodsy scent wafted over her, soaking and soothing her soul. But that lack of peace of mind she rather liked. The thrill of it made her feel all... well, she frowned, at a loss for words.

"Earth to Al."

Edin's voice abruptly brought her back to reality. She turned to face him, a lens in each hand.

She quirked her eyebrows. "What?"

"I was talking to you and you didn't hear me."

"Sorry. I was thinking about this." She waved her hand to indicate the open cargo cases littering the pool deck.

Edin ran his hand across the foam of a nearby case and gently pulled the Leica V-Lux2 from its bed. He turned it over in his hands before looking back at her. "I've never seen you so focused on something so second nature to you."

"Really?" Alexandria's spine straightened. "I wasn't aware you'd had the opportunity to watch me work."

"I'm sorry." Edin sighed. "I didn't mean to upset you." He waved his hand at the cases. "To me, this has always seemed as easy as breathing to you. I can't imagine you so focused on it." He watched her, his gaze intense. "I actually just wanted to talk. We haven't had much time for you and me to just talk."

Alexandria eased the Otus 1.4/55 lens into its foam shroud and moved to sit on the edge of a lounger, stretching her legs out before her. "Talk or advise, lecture, and remonstrate?"

Edin shrugged, slipped the Leica into its place and sat beside Alexandria on the lounge. He playfully bumped her shoulder with his, his eyes wide and innocent. "When have I ever advised, lectured, or remonstrated you?"

Alexandria bumped back but gave him a cheeky grin. "Remember Wesley Morgan?" Edin's blue eyes opened wider and his look of mock affront made Alexandria giggle.

Edin smoothed his features into a blank canvas. "Of course, I remember him. He was nothing but trouble and only wanted to get in your pants. As your brother, it was my duty to act on my knowledge."

Alexandria continued to laugh, wiping the tears from her eyes. "Really? It was your duty to duct tape him buck-naked to a flagpole in the winter?"

"Truly, the innocent young female population had every right to know what little they were bargaining for..." Edin's statement died, and he turned to stare at her. "Wait, number one: how did you know? Number two: why didn't I ever realize you weren't upset over it? You so adamantly defended him when I told you not to go out with him."

Alexandria gave him a sardonic look. "Number one: you might be a great attorney, but your foray into collegiate petty crime was pathetic—everyone knew it was you and Rudy. Nobody ever said anything because Wesley was a douche. Number two: I wasn't upset because I never did date him. You just jumped to that conclusion because you heard he asked me out. Number three: it just proves my point—you have a history of advising where you don't know the whole picture." She gently slapped him upside the back of his head to drive the point home.

Edin turned serious. "Then paint me a picture here, so I can do the right thing."

The doors closed on the cage Edin had set for her. She turned her face to stare out at the horizon. When a large warm hand clapped her on the back, she almost jumped out of her skin.

"What are you two doing out here, looking all serious?" John asked. He leaned down to kiss Alexandria's brow, "Hey, honey," while ruffling Edin's hair with his other hand.

Edin smiled. "Just catching up. We were talking about Al's little project here." He waved his hand to indicate the pool deck. "The Hollywood paparazzi need to take notes."

John walked past them and pulled a teak armchair around to face the lounge. "Really?"

Alexandria turned toward them both, her decision made. "No. Actually, Edin was preparing to lecture me on God knows what, probably the inadvisability of being in any kind of close proximity to Declan."

Momentarily speechless from her bold comment, both men stared at her. She pressed her advantage. "Before either of you say a word, I need you to listen to me. For once, I really truly need you to listen. Especially if you don't want me to disappear after the wedding."

John and Edin looked at each other and back toward Alexandria. Both nodded.

Impressed they hadn't started talking, Alexandria made her move. "I love you both, you've always been there for me, for anything I needed. But right now, I need you to hear what I have to say and not jump up and run off to fix anything or everything as you see fit. I need you to respect me."

John snapped, "Respect you! You think we don't respect you?"

Edin opened his mouth but, at Alexandria's look, he shut it.

Alexandria laid her hand gently on her father's knee. The hurt in his eyes tore at her heart. "Daddy, you respect me in every way but one—you don't trust me to survive or grow from my mistakes. You both have always been right there to fix things before they could even happen to me."

John took her hand in his. "We like to help you."

Edin bumped her shoulder. "Yeah, what are big brothers for, if not to interfere in baby sis's love life?"

With her free hand, Alexandria pulled Edin's hand to her lap. "I love you both so much. I'm so sorry I hurt you when I left...and I won't discuss why I left. At the time, I thought it was the best thing I could do for everyone."

She watched them exchange glances before looking back to her. Her teeth worried her lower lip. "I didn't realize until I left, but there was something else, something more important. Something I didn't want to face then."

Her voice softened and she looked down at their hands. "All my life, you both told me I could do anything if I put my mind to it, but what you really meant was I could do anything I wanted to if it was something you agreed with."

"That's not true!" John said.

"Dad, it is, but not in the way you're taking it. You both always supported my love of photography, but in your hearts, you wanted me close by, shooting weddings and doing studio work. Every time an offer came in for expedition work, you would put a handful of offers for local, steady work in front of me, telling me how much better they were. Edin, I think you single handedly lined up every person you ever met who was getting married to be my client. Which, by the way, was quite a feat."

John cleared his throat. "We only wanted your happiness and success. We just wanted to help."

"I know. But you never gave me the opportunity to grow, to struggle for what I wanted, and to learn to fight for my dreams." She looked to her father. "Dad, you built a shipping empire from nothing and bought an island. That's amazing."

She turned her face toward Edin. "And you, top of your class, youngest junior partner in one of the most powerful law firms in the world. You both achieved your dreams, and I wanted the chance to achieve mine, with no frills, interference, or assistance."

Edin glanced from John to Alexandria. "You could have just said so."

She smiled. "No, I couldn't. Even now, you are both

struggling with letting me make choices. You told Declan to stay away from me. You are both prepared to run interference with Brent, if you think I need it. Which, by the way, I don't."

Both men started to deny her, but at the look on her face, their shoulders dropped. Her dad spoke for them both. "We love you. It's our job to protect you."

"No, it's not. Your job was to teach me to make good decisions and you did that--even though you don't see it."

Edin looked at their hands, still on Alexandria's knees, glanced to their father and back to stare directly in her eyes. "So...what are you looking for from us?"

"I want you to let me fail."

John opened his mouth, shaking his head.

"Dad, please. I need to have the freedom to choose. Hopefully, I'll choose well, and I won't fall on my face. But if I don't, I need to know I can cope with falling."

She stared from one to another, both so alike. She loved them so much, her heart squeezed, lungs constricted as she awaited their answers.

Dad's lips formed a firm line, but he nodded.

Edin smiled his agreement

CHAPTER EIGHTEEN

"She does know we're here looking for whale sharks, not big-titted bimbos, right?" Rosamund's sarcastic tone sent gales of laughter through the four women sitting shoulder to shoulder on the swim deck of the Monterey bowrider.

Meredith pressed her lips together. "I can't believe Victor brought her here. She's such a bitch. What does he see in her?"

"I'm sure double-D slut behavior has nothing to do with it," Leann reasoned.

"If that's the case, if he can't keep her in his room, at least he could keep his bitch on a leash." Meredith's words dripped with acid. "I mean, they hardly speak to one another. She definitely doesn't speak to us, unless she's making snarky remarks, so why is she even here?"

Alexandria looked at the three women to her right, smiled wryly, and turned back to watch the object of their feline banter. From the swim deck of the other bowrider anchored a short swim away, Louisa postured in her barely-there gold lamé bikini which left very little to the imagination.

Alexandria had spent enough time in the Serengeti with wild animals on the hunt to know a predator when she saw one. This particular predator had left no doubt as to the object of her chase. The mystery was why Victor agreed to bring her, when she so obviously was here to pursue Declan.

Alexandria paused the can of ginger ale at her lips, "She's not here after any of your men, so you can all relax." She took a deep drink to gather her thoughts.

Three pairs of surprised eyes turned to her. Meredith took the lead. "We all know that. She's after your man. Which just pisses *us* off."

Alexandria choked on her mouthful of soda.

Leann leaned over to pound her on the back.

Since when had Declan become her man in their eyes? She stared at Meredith. For that matter, when had *she* started thinking of him as hers?

Leann and Rosamund leaned in close to Meredith. Meredith looked at her. "Are you going to stake your claim, or leave him to her mercy?"

Three wicked smiles clearly indicated their preference.

Crystalline blue water pushed and pulled Declan's body, making him sway in time with the tidal flow. A group of dark blue, juvenile emperor angel fish with their electric blue and white rings were upstaged as a mandarin fish glided across the field of vision in his snorkel mask, its brilliant blue and orange patterned body with neon yellow accents screaming "'look at me."

A tap on his shoulder. He turned to see Edin indicate with a quick jerk of his thumb that he was going topside.

Declan wished he didn't have to surface for air at all. Here in this quiet, peaceful blue world he could pretend Louisa wasn't circling like a great white shark, and he could let thoughts of Alexandria and her passion swirl around him like the silken waters.

As he kicked toward the brightness of the surface, Declan's mind churned. He could easily see the bottoms of the two bowriders anchored not too far from the outer reef that encircled the wide, rounded end of the island. Three pair of dainty feet and the lower half of Edin's body dangled in the water from one swim deck.

Through the clear waters, he could see Louisa standing on the other. He angled closer to the boat of many feet. Bad enough that he had been trapped with Louisa and Victor on the outbound trip, he wasn't getting back on it when it looked like she was the only occupant. Stupid was not his middle name.

He was just about to break the surface when Alexandria's lithe body sliced through the waters in a clean dive. Declan watched her turn gracefully in the water, like a fit sea nymph, to face him.

Her eyes were open, a smile on her face. She kicked up close beside him.

Together, they broke the surface of the water.

"I was coming to save you." The softly spoken words caressed his ears.

He smiled, puzzled. "Appreciate that, but from what?"

"Apparently, there has been a sighting of a new breed of man-eating, big-titted bimbo shark in our local waters. Our rescue team was a little worried for your welfare."

Laughter erupted from the boat, and Edin leaned over the low gunwale. "If I were you, I would accept the rescue and hold on tight."

Declan's heart squeezed. He couldn't remember the last time someone had tried to look out for him, much less rescue him. An unfamiliar sense of yearning filled him, making him wish he belonged here, and for the first time making him realize how solitary his life had become these past years.

Using his left hand to anchor him to the swim deck, he faced Alexandria, who floated closer. Her hand glided up his ribs and chest to his shoulder, tethering her to him, leaving a trail of gooseflesh where her hand had been.

His groin tightened with desire and he tried not to think of her long beautiful body encased in a thin sheath of sapphire blue Lycra, less than an arm's length away.

Whoever said one-piece swimsuits were for old ladies had never seen Alexandria. It hugged her body in all the right places, and the Grecian cut front was a thousand times more subtly sexual than the porn star suit Louisa strutted about in on the other boat.

A wave of water splashed over Declan from behind. Alexandria laughed and wiped her face with her free hand while Declan turned to a grinning Rudy.

Leann slid from the swim deck into the warm tropical water. "You two better appreciate this sacrifice."

Rudy pulled a face. "Yeah, we're taking one for the team here."

Alexandria chuckled. "Believe me, we do and will." She moved closer in the water and rested her chin on Declan's shoulder as Rudy and Leann pushed off from the swim deck and headed to the other bowrider.

Her voice sent tingles down his spine. "They're riding back with Louisa." Declan glanced toward Louisa. Her cold, calculated smile sent chills of a different nature down his spine.

CHAPTER NINETEEN

Declan watched as Edin, with two bottles of Paulaner Wiesn Bier in each hand, closed the mini-fridge with his foot and set to opening the bottles. He passed one each to Declan, Rudy, and Victor. They clinked in a silent toast and took long pulls on the cold, sparkling brew. In a handful of moments beads of sweat ran down the neck of the ice cold Wiesn.

The warm offshore breeze was a welcome respite to the muggy afternoon heat. Between the frosty beer, the rising breeze, and Rudy's quick humor, the tension pulling Declan's spine into a steel rod was letting up.

Rudy possessed a wicked sense of humor, which Dec appreciated. Since their chance meeting in the jungle, he had come to appreciate the man's integrity and intelligence, as well. But he wasn't used to making friends for the sake of friendship. Everyone he knew was somehow linked to the business empire his father had thrust into his hands. Even his friendship with Edin had come from that source.

As he realized he felt out of his element, a wry hint of a smile tickled at his lips. That wasn't a feeling he was used to, but then, since coming to this damn island for some peace and quiet, he had found himself flipped end over ass by an Amazonian girl/woman, hunted like big prey and hell...just spun every which way from normal.

He listened to the end of Rudy's joke and laughed as he delivered his witty punch-line. As the laughter died, his gaze caught Victor's. *Aw, what the hell?*

"Hey, Vic." Declan drew his full attention.

"Yeah."

"Don't mean to start any shit, but what's the deal with Louisa? Do you think you could shorten her leash? She's here with you but seems to be chasing me. No offense intended."

Victor laughed bitterly. "No offense taken." He glanced aside to Edin. "I should just apologize all the way around. If I could get that bitch off the island right now, I'd do it."

Edin peered at his friend. "I don't get it. I didn't even know you were dating her."

Victor gagged on his beer, coughing to clear his throat. "I'm not. Matter of fact, I'd like to choke her with that leash." He looked at his audience and flushed. "I don't know where the hell that woman gets her intel—but it's top shelf."

He looked at Declan but indicated Rudy and Edin, pointing with his beer bottle. "These two can vouch for this. A couple of months ago, she shows up out of the blue and starts hanging out at some of the places we frequent. Not actually up in anyone's face, but she's hard to miss in a crowd."

Rudy nodded. "Aye, that much is true. Don't ever tell Leann she was right, but she told me that bitch was on the hunt and she felt sorry for her target."

Victor blew out a heavy sigh. "Yeah, well, I'm not the

target, as you've gathered," he looked to Declan, "but that woman has gone to enormous lengths to get to you."

Edin's bottle hit the bar with a crack. "Fine, she's a bitch, she's on safari for Dec here, but why the hell did you bring her to the island? It's my fuckin' wedding and I don't want to deal with her."

Victor's shoulders sank. "I'm sorry. I'm sorry for everything, but I didn't have a choice."

"What, she had a gun? Does she holster it between the big tits? Or can she hide it in the overly loose muffin?"

Rudy's wide-eyed mockery created a vision of Louisa armed that Declan wished he could laugh off. He felt an uncommon sympathy for Victor. "Louisa is a viper. I'm sure the shit runs deeper than even he knows."

Victor scanned his audience. "That's an understatement." Sighing, he shook his head. "My idiot of a brother has been banging some college. If his wife finds out, she'll have him and the family business by the balls. I don't know how Louisa got a hold of it, but that was her leverage to get here. I'm sorry."

"Well, fuck me," Edin said. "That blows." He indicated Dec with a point of his beer. "Are you sure you'll get free and clear if she doesn't nail our friend here?"

"He won't." Before Victor could reply, Declan spoke. "It's more than likely that if your brother has been banging this chick for a short while, Louisa herself baited the trap to get the ammo she needed to get here. How long has your brother been getting screwed?"

"A few months, maybe?"

Declan turned to Edin. "I accepted your invitation in early August, so the timing coincides. Louisa tried to contact me in July, and I refused the bait." Three startled gazes turned to him.

"You haven't exactly explained how you know her or why she's so obviously hunting you." Edin spoke.

Declan's jaw tightened. "And I'm not going to." His tone went cold. "As far as I'm concerned, she's dead and buried and can stay that way." He looked at the three men facing him. "I think the critical thing now is to get her off this island and find a way to neutralize anything she has on Vic's brother."

"I'll call my partner." Tom's quiet voice captured their attention. "He's an expert in..." Tom paused, "shall we say, specialized investigations?"

"Tossing her in the ocean isn't an option?" Rudy inquired.

Declan smiled. "That would be easy and convenient, but seeing as how our friend Edin here is an officer of the court and bound by law, we don't want him going up the river for murder."

Edin twirled his bottle between his fingers and looked at them from under lowered brows. "In international waters, the captain of a vessel holds the power of life and death over passengers. Let's take her out to sea and chuck her overboard."

Declan laughed. "Sorry, Edin, maritime laws have changed since the 1700. We'll have to deal with her some other way. You're no pirate. Besides, she'd probably terrorize some poor great white into bringing her back."

CHAPTER TWENTY

The early morning sun glanced off the cream-colored marble counters of Margaret's kitchen. With her hair up and her bare feet sliding across the basil colored cushiony rubber flooring as she whipped and mixed, Margaret didn't feel old enough to be a stepmother of grown adults.

A smile played on her lips, but as arms ensnared her in a quick hug from behind, she let out a startled yelp. Margaret almost dropped the half gallon of milk in her hand.

The arms fell away and she turned to see a smiling Alexandria. "My goodness, child, what's this about?"

She set the milk on the counter and moved to the kitchen island to pull a net bag of mangos from an overhead hook.

Alexandria laughed. "I thought I would stop in and spend a little time with you." She popped a blueberry from the produce box into her mouth and pulled a stool over to sit by the counter. "Do you need any help?"

Margaret smiled. "Gracious, no. Everything was mostly completed by the staff last night. I'm just putting things together and baking the coffee cakes. Today, it's an easy breezy buffet."

"Margaret?"

Alexandria's tone stopped Margaret in her tracks, and she turned to face her stepdaughter. "What is it honey?"

Tears bloomed in Alexandria's eyes. "I'm so sorry I wasn't there when you and Dad got married."

Margaret plopped the bag of mangos to the counter and moved to enfold her in a tight hug. She kissed her step-daughter's temple before leaning back to cup Al's cheek with the palm of her hand.

Alexandria's tears spilled down her cheeks. "I've been so thoughtless...and selfish."

"Shush, sweetheart." Margaret's hands stroked her hair and tucked her close. She closed her eyes, savoring the feel of the daughter in her arms. She might not have given her birth, but she had watched her take her first steps. She pulled back to look Alexandria in the eyes, pausing to brush the tears away. "What is this about?"

"I wasn't there..." Alexandria looked out the garden window to the sunlit skies beyond. She breathed deep and turned to face Margaret. "You've always been there for us...for me. You and James were part of our family, and I wasn't there..."

Margaret pulled another stool over and perched close enough to hold Alexandria's hands. She smiled at her step-daughter, in so many ways still a woman-child. "Honey, sometimes the luckiest ones are the ones who get to pick their family. James and I were best friends with your mom and dad from grade school. We always felt more a part of their families than our own—so we were the lucky ones. We picked the family we wanted to belong to. I would have liked you to be there, but I understood why you weren't."

Alexandria frowned. "What do you mean?"

"Losing Caterina only a year after my James passed was hell." She sighed, lost in memory for a moment. "But I never believed you left because of her death. You've always been so protective of others and loyal to a fault. I may not know the exact reasons, but I'm sure it has more to do with Brent and less with anything else."

Alexandria's mouth formed an "o" but no sound came out. She closed her mouth. "Have you said anything to Dad?"

The backs of Margaret's fingers stroked Alexandria's face. "Your secrets are yours to tell, my love."

"Who has secrets?"

John's loud voice in the early morning made both women jump.

"Good grief, John! You nearly made me jump out of my skin." Margaret came to her feet, pushing the stool back to the bar edge. "How long have you been hovering?"

John walked to the coffee bar, followed by a yawning Edin. "I wasn't hovering. We just wanted some coffee. What are you two up to in here?" Both men looked at them, eyebrows raised in matching expressions.

Alexandria gazed at the three people she loved the most in the world.

Edin ambled over to the coffee bar and pulled down two mugs, his hand on a third. He turned to her. "Coffee?"

She nodded, swallowing the hard lump in her throat. It seemed like her life had become all about lies, deception, and hurt. She was so sick of it all. Maybe it was time to go on offense here, as well as with Brent. She moved to help Edin with the coffee. "Anybody else awake?"

Edin laughed. "Hardly. God love her, but Meredith was snoring like a yak when I left, and the guest wing was like a tomb when I went by there."

John walked behind her as he took a stool next to his wife. "Well, if your pals weren't pounding shots until four a.m. maybe they would be up."

Edin grinned and moved to the island, sliding a steaming mug of coffee to his dad.

Alexandria followed and slipped onto a stool between her brother and father, sipping the warm brew. Although, with as much French vanilla creamer as she used, she wasn't sure it qualified as real coffee.

Her gaze caught Margaret's, who gave her an encouraging nod. Al smiled. "So, what's the opposite of a bedtime story? A wakeup story?"

Edin made a face. "Right. Usually they are called board meetings and they put you back to sleep."

She glanced at Dad and Edin. "Well, whatever you call it, I have one for you. Do you remember the day I came to your office and broke off the engagement with Brent?"

"Of course, it shocked the shit out of me."

"I'm sure you were no more shocked than I was when I went by his apartment and found him screwing some woman."

Both men flushed and started to rise.

But she was ready for them. She grabbed a forearm on each side of her. "Stop! Sit down and listen."

"That lying, cheating little bastard." John mumbled.

A game plan of vengeance written all over his face. "Knock it off," Alexandria said. "I found him with her on Friday night, the night I was supposed to be shooting the wedding rehearsal for the Orris-DeBarros wedding. I was pissed and left for Manitowoc that night. I spent the weekend staring at the lake and thinking about my life. All weekend, Brent kept up a constant stream of voice-mails and emails, vacillating between begging me to come back and threatening you both if I went public with what happened. Maybe it wasn't the best solution, but I'd gotten the offer from Barron's to shoot the Greenland scenes and it left in two weeks. They were just waiting for me to answer. I knew that if I told either of you what happened, you would react just like you started to now. You would storm out, find Brent, beat the shit out of him, and cause all kinds of problems with Edin's career, your business ties with the law firm. All kinds of things."

"You think any of that would matter?" Reproach and anger tainted Edin's voice.

"It mattered to me. Plus, there was something I didn't want to face then." Her voice softened, and she hooked her arms through theirs, leaning over to kiss first one, then the other on the cheek. Smiling at them both, she re-grouped her thoughts. "We already discussed your innate desire to pave the way and protect me—even from myself."

John looked at Margaret. "You knew this, and you didn't say anything?"

She smiled. "Not for sure, but I figured there was more to the story. Caterina and I never thought Brent was worthy of Al, but like I always say...it wasn't my secret to tell."

John frowned as his frequently chanted mantra came back around.

Alexandria shook her head from side to side. "Even after our agreement at the pool, you are both struggling with letting me make choices. You told Declan to stay away from me and you are both prepared to go find Brent and beat the shit out of him."

Edin stroked the back of her hand where it lay on his forearm. "To think I introduced you to Brent."

"And I'm glad you did."

Both men snapped their gazes to Alexandria's face and pulled their hands free, curling their fists on their knees.

"Bullshit," John said flatly.

The look on his face indicated he had plans for Brent. Alexandria smiled. "Actually, you might want to wait on your revenge. Some things are best served cold, and he's gonna have a few surprises very soon. Plus, he didn't get that black eye from a hiking fall."

Male eyes widened, followed by snorts of laughter.

"Explain that one..." Edin said.

Alexandria rubbed her palms lightly on her knees. "He confronted me at the beach, we had words. I punched him so hard he bounced when he landed on his ass. I told him to leave me the hell alone. But I don't think that was the explanation you wanted." She took a deep breath and let it out on a long sigh. "I'm, well, maybe not happy, but...perhaps appreciative is the right word about my history with Brent. However, I am glad that you insisted I come here for the holidays."

She smiled. "If I hadn't had the experience with Brent, I might never have pursued my real dream of earning my own place in the world, being independent, traveling, my naturalist work, and sharing the world my photography opens up with others. I might have gone along just being a Real Housewife of Chicago or something. But being here now makes me realize that I'm never letting go of our family again. I'm really sorry for the pain I caused. I did think I was protecting our family as a whole."

John cleared his throat. "Honey, I'm sorry, too. Maybe, if we had paid more attention, we could have avoided all this heartache."

Edin agreed. "Yeah, and perhaps we should make a pact to address anything that comes up together, respecting each other's opinions and wishes." He looked at his dad, who nodded, and back to Alexandria. "However, Dad and I get at least a shot at Brent for hurting you."

She held up her hands. "Oh, I don't think so. Until I arrived here, it never occurred to me that when all the shit hit the fan with him—I was angry, pissed, betrayed—I can't even tell you the range of things that crossed my mind. But it wasn't until now, that I realized that not once was I ever broken hearted. That has to say something, like maybe I dodged a bullet?"

Edin's arm went around her shoulders, and he kissed her temple. "I'm sorry for what you went through--and alone, at that." He looked at this dad. "But I still think Brent and I should have a little conversation—at the very least."

She threw them a mischievous smile. "Well, you may have to get in line. His dad is on his way here to collect him, and based on my conversation with Carl, I think he would prefer your fists to his dad."

Both men stared at her.

"What did you do?" Edin asked.

"I called Carl and gave him a complete rundown on Brent's antics, including the last four years of psycho emails and phone calls. He was pretty pissed." Alexandria took a sip of coffee.

"Carl didn't build one of the largest law practices in the nation by losing clients. And since he started opening offices internationally, he can't afford any bad press. If the firm lost our account," she looked from John to Edin, "or you, for that matter, it would hurt."

She smiled. "I believe his exact words were, 'I'll be there shortly to collect him and relocate him to his new assignment.' Carl was telling me he just opened an office in Nuuk, Greenland. Apparently, between mineral rights and the new push for oil and natural gas explorations, the market for legal services is expanding."

Howls of laughter erupted.

Edin brushed tears from his eyes, and he turned to his sister. "Baby sis, remind me to never piss you off. Holy shit. Fucking Greenland. He'll freeze off what little balls he has."

John stood and pulled them all into a big family hug. "By God, your mother would be so proud."

CHAPTER TWENTY-ONE

Brent stood before the floor-to-ceiling windows of his bedroom; his hands tightly fisted at his sides. He stared, unseeing, at the sunlight streaming through the coral-colored clouds, showering the horizon with golden beams of light. Something warm and wet trickled down his palm, tickling his hand. Glancing down, he watched drops of blood drip onto the pale beige Berber carpet.

Opening his fist, the broken glass fell to the carpet. Flexing his fingers, he noted the skin of his palm pulling apart where the razor-sharp glass had sliced his skin. *He could fix this! That bitch. How could she do this to him?*

A sharp, insistent rapping on the door ripped his attention back to the present. He snatched a hand towel off the bathroom counter, wrapped it around his hand, and strode to the bedroom door. He yanked the door open. "What?"

"Well, well. Nice outfit." Louisa's gaze took Brent in from head to toe, lingering on the towel wrapped around his hips. She brushed past him and walked around his room. Brent shoved the door shut and turned to follow.

"So...to what do I owe the honor of this little visit? I'm on a tight schedule." His jaw locked.

As Louisa moved, her blood red fingernails dragged along the top of the dresser. "Yes, I've heard. Rumor has it Daddy is due to arrive any time." Her fingers moved to her collarbone.

They dragged his gaze with them as they slid down the deep vee of her halter dress, stroking her skin. Her hard nipples pressed against the thin fabric and her hand slid inside the halter to caress herself.

His cock twitched with heat.

Louisa's lips curled up. "I think we can help one another."

"What?" Brent's eyes narrowed. "A little see-you-off fuck between strangers?"

Sliding up, her free hand pulled the bow at the back of her neck and the two triangles of fabric slid forward. The twin globes of flesh sprang loose of their restraint. She cupped the weight of her breasts in her palms, her fingers massaging and pinching her flesh. "We each want something." She wet her lips and tilted her head slightly to the side.

He could feel her assessment, her gaze lingering on the growing bulge under his towel. He could play her game. "Go on."

Louisa moved in. Her right hand stroked his chest while, her left pulled the towel free from his hips, dropping it to the floor. She pressed the flat of her hand to his abdomen, sliding down to take his swelling cock in her hand. With the other, her finger and thumb circled his nipple before pinching the sensitive nub.

As her talons tightened around him, he sucked air.

Suddenly, she released him and stepped back, the back

of her legs against his bed. She slid her hands up the sides of her thighs slowly, hitching on the hem of her short, clinging dress, pulling the fabric higher, pausing just as the fabric revealed the pink flush of her mound. Raising a hand to her mouth, she sucked her first two fingers, then slid them into her slit, fondling and rubbing as she tilted her head back.

Brent's cock jumped to attention as he watched her play with herself. Swallowing hard, he stroked himself. "I assume there's an agenda to this sideshow."

Her eyes narrowed. "Of course. I want Declan. Alexandria is in my way. You want Alexandria. He is in your way. If we eliminate your competition, we eliminate both of our roadblocks."

Brent moved close to Louisa and roughly shoved her back on the bed, spreading her thighs and grabbing her hips, pulling her hard towards him as he slammed himself deep. "I like where this is going."

CHAPTER TWENTY-TWO

Carl Collingsworth wasn't easily impressed. But the young woman before him did just that. Her firm handshake and direct gaze that never slid away spoke volumes. His son was an idiot for letting this one get away. But, then again, he'd bailed that damn kid out of trouble so many times he ought to have no second thoughts about his mental condition.

"Thank you for coming all this way, Carl. I'm sorry it had to be under circumstances like this." The sincerity in her voice touched him.

"I'm sorry, too. Actually, for a wide variety of things: my son, his behavior, the situation it put you in. I only wish you had come to me sooner. Maybe these last years could have been easier for you."

Alexandria smiled.

Carl could see why Brent wanted her back. She was like life itself, vibrant and full of energy. A definite prize for one with the nerve to challenge and win her.

She gave him a quick hug, which startled him, and hooked her arm through his. "Why don't we talk while we walk to the house?"

Not waiting for an answer, she tugged him forward. "I appreciate your kindness, Carl, and I do regret many things about the last few years, but my experiences have helped me..." She looked at him. "Grow. And I've found out a lot about myself that maybe I wouldn't have otherwise." She smiled and looked up the trail.

Carl smiled also. "I wanted to thank you, as well, Alexandria."

"For what? Running to you like a tattletale?" She quirked her eyebrow at him.

"Actually, yes. You could have done many things—spiteful, angry things—or chosen a path that would have created more conflict. But you came to me to help you find a resolution that would have minimum impact on both your family and my firm. That took a maturity that many people don't have." He laughed. "If they did, my firm wouldn't be nearly as successful."

"Well, I wanted a win-win situation as much as possible. But I'm pretty sure that's not how Brent will see this." She grimaced. "I'm sorry about causing you any difficulty with him."

He patted her arm where it still rested on his forearm as they walked. "It's not your fault, honey. Life is full of consequences. Maybe, if I had taken him in hand a long time ago, we wouldn't be having this conversation now."

She remained quiet and thoughtful.

Maybe she felt guilty. "You have to realize, this isn't the first time I've had to clean up his messes..." Carl continued. "But this will be the last. If he doesn't straighten his act up in Nuuk, I'm tempted to disinherit him and let him fend for himself."

Her eyes widened. "Ouch. I don't see him working gas fields or fishing for a living."

"It certainly wouldn't be like living here. Quite a little hideaway your family has." As a howler monkey screamed nearby, he jumped.

She patted his arm. "Just a howler monkey telling us he is here. I thought you'd been here before?"

"I've been invited often enough. I just never seem to make the time to get away." Regret tinged his voice.

"Well, we'll have to make sure you accept future invitations." She launched into being an informative hostess, pointing out flora and fauna along the trail.

He was focused on a cascading vine bursting with purple passion fruit flowers when he felt her tug him to the right.

Carl almost laughed. As they stepped onto the pool deck, his gaze took in the line-up of males protectively hovering by the bar. John, Edin, Declan, and Edin's friend, Rudy, were practically frothing at the mouth. He whispered to Alexandria, "How did you get free to meet me alone?"

"It wasn't easy," she remarked. "What convincing wouldn't do, threatening had to handle."

Carl chuckled. "Boy, what I could accomplish with you on my team." He patted her hand before releasing her and heading toward John. Shaking his right hand, he smacked John on the shoulder with his other hand. "That is one helluva daughter you've got there, John."

John smiled, although it didn't quite reach his eyes. "I think so. It's been a while, Carl," he said as he pumped Carl's hand.

Carl's lips thinned. No sense in beating around the bush. "Ugly business, this. I'm sorry. I didn't know and, when Alexandria called me, I just knew I had to come. Try to make things right."

John smiled again, a real smile. "We appreciate it. It was

a long trip. Would you like a drink?" He moved behind the bar and waited for Carl's request.

"Whiskey? Neat?" He watched as John poured a fifteen-year-old Powers Irish Special into a Glencairn whisky glass and, upon nods from the others, set up rounds for each man. The fine amber liquid beckoned him.

Alexandria slipped behind the bar next to her dad, pulled a Shocktop Honeycrisp Apple beer, and popped the top.

John raised his glass in a toast. "Here's to resolving the past and putting it behind us."

Carl clinked his glass in agreement, and slowly sipped the fine brew. An appreciative sigh left him.

John turned his attention back to Carl. "How is your timing, Carl? We've plenty of space if you want to stay over and rest a bit? Or, at the very least, stay for dinner?"

"That's good of you, John, but all things considered, I think it would be best to collect Brent and let your family get back to celebrating the holidays. The jet is waiting in Saipan and we have some more flying yet to do."

"Really?" Brent's caustic voice cut through the thick afternoon air. "Are we in a hurry to get back to Chicago, Dad?"

Looking his son up and down, Carl smiled. "I hope you packed warmer clothes than shorts and sandals. Nice shiner, son. Where'd you get that?" Knowing full well the answer, he couldn't help the dig.

Brent's neck flushed red and his hand went to his cheek, gingerly pressing the black and purple flesh that circled up and around his left eye. "I fell when I was hiking...hit a tree." He looked at Alexandria. "May I speak to you, Al?"

Before Alexandria could respond, Declan moved between them.

John and Edin rose on either side.

She moved quickly to the forefront, stalling them, her hand on Declan's forearm. "I don't know what else there is to say, Brent."

Brent looked from the protective circle at her back to his dad. The condemnation there was no surprise. It wasn't like the old bastard had ever been there for him. Why couldn't he just knock off? "Please, Al. Just a moment of your time."

She nodded and moved to step forward.

Declan's voice stopped her. "Stay within sight."

She raised her brows at his edict.

He had the good grace to step back. "Please."

She smiled. "There's no reason not to. Just relax."

Brent smirked at Declan as he turned to follow her to the other side of the pool, near the jungle's edge.

She spun abruptly and crossed her arms to face him.

Her confidence irked him, and he stared. He so wanted to wipe it away, to take everything from her and put her where she belonged—at his command.

"Well?"

Brent shook himself. "Well, what?"

"You said you had something to say, so please get to it. I don't know how long they'll actually stay out of earshot." She glanced to the array of agitated men standing by the bar.

"Right, then. Aw...I handled everything so badly, Al. I wanted to say I'm sorry."

"You're sorry." She searched his face. "That's it?"

The words stung. The acid in her tone eating away at his last layer of hesitation. *Remember the plan.* He shoved his hands into his pockets and rocked on his heels.

"No." He glanced into the jungle and back to her. "No, that's not all. Al, you've condemned me for being a cheat and a womanizer, but now you're involved with Ruaidhrí. His reputation is worse than mine. He's just like me. You just haven't caught him yet."

Her gaze hardened.

He backtracked. "Please, just listen. I'm warning you. I don't want you to be hurt again."

"I'm fully capable of taking care of myself, Brent." The frost in her voice cooled the air between them.

"I'm sure you are. Frankly, I'm surprised your dad and Edin even let him near you. Especially since they are familiar with his stunts. I mean, he lost his fiancée because of his womanizing and he's being sued by the family of his lover who committed suicide over his treatment of her."

The shock on her face was pay dirt, and he knew it. Hopefully, she wouldn't pry too deeply into those claims, or she'd find the lies. All he needed to do was plant the seed. Louisa would do the rest. When she made good on her promises, Al would be begging him to take her back.

Now, to fertilize the seed. "Al, I made the biggest mistake of my life when I let you down. I want to make amends. Please, be careful where he's concerned." He wasn't sure she had even heard his words until she nodded, turned, and walked back to the bar.

He followed, giving Declan a sneer as he stalked past, ignoring Edin and John to stop before his dad. "Well, let's get this party started." He smiled at the words and headed down the trail, leaving his father to make his own way to the docks. The fools behind him had no idea what party had just been set in motion.

CHAPTER TWENTY-THREE

Louisa reclined on the deck chair filing her long nails lazily. The wide-brimmed hat and dark shades hid her sharp gaze. The huddle of men at the bar seemed deep in conversation, glancing at her every now and again.

Apparently, Victor had spilled his guts and they were looking for ways to remedy his problems. Other than blackmailing Victor into bringing her here, she couldn't be tied to the shit storm brewing in Chicago. Charlene had that project well in hand. She nearly laughed.

She turned her attention to the four women chatting on the steps in the shallow end, drinking their fruity, snooty cocktails. Dismissing all but one, she focused her attention on Alexandria. That little bitch would get her comeuppance shortly.

Meredith repeated her question to Alexandria.

The poor girl seemed quite distracted.

Louisa cracked a smile. She could see the doubts blooming, little by little in the warm afternoon sun, fed by girl talk and gossip of boyfriends past.

She checked her watch. If all was going as planned in

the states, Vic's dumb-shit brother would be discovering his wife's body soon. The poor, childless woman who took her life when she was replaced in her husband's affection by a younger, more beautiful woman, who carried his heir.

From the corner of her eye, Alexandria saw Declan smile at one of Rudy's endless jokes, and her stomach did a flip kick against her spine. She leaned back on the shallow steps, let her head rest on the pool edge, and tried to find peace of mind. Even with Brent's departure, her unease was riding high.

Behind her polarized Oakley's, her gaze followed two Christmas Shearwaters as they glided overhead, gently beating their chocolate brown wings and calling to each other as they turned toward the cliffs. Their calls echoed across cloudless azure skies and she smiled at the fluke of viewing the rarely seen fowl during Christmas week.

The fronds of the palms at the edge of the pool ruffled in the afternoon breeze. Any given day of the week, this scene was her special recipe for inner peace, but today, she just couldn't find her groove.

Meredith, Leann, and Rosamund were floating on rafts at the deep end but she felt no motivation to join them. Their talk of husbands, or in Mere's case her fiancé, left her feeling out of touch. With a turn of her head, she saw Margaret and her dad heading into the theatre room for an afternoon of movies.

She sighed. Everyone was in pairs—well, not quite everyone. Louisa flounced to her feet and stretched widely, drawing eyes from around the deck.

At the sight, a tide of anger rose in Alexandria. The

bitter taste of bile made her want to vomit. The woman was vile, just horrendous and tacky beyond belief. The animal print bikini she was sporting today tied at the sides and barely covered anything. So far, Margaret and Dad hadn't made a fuss, but they had to be offended by her.

Unable to look at her another minute, Alexandria came to her feet and strode from the pool to the deck chair, hastily wrapping her towel around herself and snatching up her flip-flops, then made for the kitchen.

Alexandria dropped her flip-flops on the floor in front of the fridge and opened the door to peruse her options. As she contemplated the consequences of cold, sweet mango versus cheesecake, she wiggled her feet into her flip-flops. Sighing, she realized neither sounded appealing, so she slammed the door only to find Louisa leaning against the counter.

"What's wrong? Nothing quite measuring up?" Louisa asked.

"Excuse me?"

"You seem...frustrated. I just thought maybe you couldn't figure out what you wanted." She pushed away from the counter to the in-island drink fridge and pulled a diet Coke from the shelf. She popped the top and took a leisurely sip.

Alexandria eyed her warily. In the days since her arrival, Louisa had never spoken directly to her. For that matter, she couldn't place a time when she had heard Louisa have a conversation with anyone. She just seemed to always be there, like that spider in the garden just waiting for her prey to come within reach.

Louisa's lips spread in a sly grin. "I, myself, always know what I want...and I always get what I want."

"Really? That doesn't seem to be working so well for you

right now." Acid churned in Alexandria's stomach. She leaned against the cool refrigerator in the hope the nausea would subside.

"He's just mad. He'll get over it." Louisa looked at her slyly. "Did he tell you we are engaged?" She pulled the gold chain she wore away from her skin, and an engagement ring popped out of the depths of her abundant cleavage.

Alexandria watched the ring sway on the chain. *How in the hell do you hide a five-carat engagement ring between your boobs?* "No, I don't believe he mentioned you." At least, not by name.

Louisa sighed. "I'm not surprised. After what he put me through, and that nasty little legal matter, he wasn't much fun, and he certainly didn't like getting a dose of his own medicine."

Irritation beat trepidation into submission. Alexandria stood tall. "I don't know where you're going, but why don't you just get there?"

Louisa tilted her head, regarding Alexandria. "Okay. We are engaged. When I caught him in bed with some college co-ed, I was livid. I was ready to break it off, but he begged me to reconsider, so I did. He's the love of my life, and I couldn't tell him no. But I couldn't let him off the hook that easy, either. So, he got a dose of his own medicine when I paid him back in kind. I let him catch me in bed with one of his competitors, and even though he knows he deserved it, his pride made him walk away. Then that stupid co-ed killed herself and all the nasty legal business started, just when we were working things out."

Declan's remarks on the plane about a couple of tough years teased the back of her mind. "What has this to do with me?"

"Entertainment, darling." Louisa sipped her Coke. "He

wants me to prove how much I love him and to what lengths I'll go to get him back. He is toying with you to make me jealous."

Alexandria considered the woman before her. "I think you've made a serious mistake."

Louisa tucked the ring back between her breasts. "How so?"

Alexandria walked past Louisa to the door. "He's a good man, and he deserves better than you. He's not a fool to be played."

As she watched Alexandria turn on her heel and march out of the kitchen, Louisa's eyes narrowed and her jaw clenched. *Well, the brat has some spunk. Good thing she has to die to make this plan work.*

CHAPTER TWENTY-FOUR

Steam clouded the white marble shower stall. Rivulets of condensation snaked their way down the glass door, leaving clear trails in their wake. Head bent forward, her hands braced on the shower walls, Alexandria let the hot water pound her head and shoulders, the heat making her skin rosy and flushed.

Her fingers curling in frustration on the hard stone, she turned and leaned against the marble, only to slide down to the floor and wrap her arms around her knees. Her head sagged forward and she rested her forehead on her arms.

Thoughts swirled in her head, as vague and hard to grasp as the tendrils of mist rising around her. She breathed a deep lungful of warm, moist air and leaned her head back against the wall, eyes closed, and sat for a handful of moments. But the persistent restlessness wouldn't let up.

Resolutely, she opened her eyes and rose, shut off the shower, and wrapped herself in a large, fluffy towel. Grabbing a second, she padded to the window wall and stood looking at the starlit sky as she used the second towel to rub the water from her hair.

Pensive, she turned and caught her reflection in the mirror. A wry smile curved her lips. She looked just like she did every other day. Tall, too thin, crazy red hair. *So, why don't I feel the same?* All her words of the last few days flew through her head. Her fight with Dad and Edin to stand down and allow her to handle Brent, to make her own choices, to have her confessions as well as her realizations. So much turmoil and emotional upheaval swirled within her, as she stared at her reflection.

Sinking to the sapphire blue chaise lounge, she played each day since she left Chicago over in her mind. Images of Declan bombarded her: sending that sweaty pig up to first class, getting rid of the annoying flirt, his confidences given, his support upon Brent's arrival, as well as his departure. With every image her heartbeat slowed. Her mind calmed. She took a deep breath and, as she exhaled she felt a sea of serenity wash over her. Clarity came like a stream of light from a lighthouse. Her images of Declan were so far removed from the pictures painted by Dad, Edin, and Louisa. She couldn't reconcile her Declan with theirs. The realization that she didn't want to freed her. She knew what she wanted; now all she had to do was go get it.

Declan sat on the side of his bed, his forearms resting on his knees as he leaned forward, contemplating the coming sunrise. He blew out a strong breath and rubbed one hand over the back of his neck, trying to massage the tension away. A storm was coming, and he wasn't sure how to avoid it.

He wasn't a big believer in coincidence, and where Louisa went, shit was sure to follow. Seeing her had shocked him. Why and how she had hooked up with this crowd to get to him he didn't know, but it didn't bode well for Victor or his family. *Well, better Victor than me.*

Then there was the little matter of a red-headed vixen who turned him inside out and made him feel things he didn't want to feel. Any foolish boyhood dreams of a happy family laughing around the Christmas tree had died long ago. Lost in thought, he almost didn't hear the soft tapping at his door.

As he reached for the knob, he stopped, uncertain. He certainly didn't want to answer if it was Louisa. When the tapping came again, he moved close to the door.

Alexandria's soft voice called through the door. "Declan?"

He opened the door quick and quiet, the pre-dawn visit revving up his protective instincts. "Al, are you okay?" he whispered.

Alexandria, fully dressed and trail ready, was smiling. "Yeah, can you meet me at the waterfall on the main trail in twenty minutes?"

Her husky whisper was warm honey to his ears. Alexandria's once-over reminded him he was wearing nothing but boxer shorts, and his cock jumped in awareness. "Yeah, but do you just want to wait? We'll go together."

"No, I've got to do something quick and I'll meet you there."

She slipped away before he could protest. He could hardly follow her around the island in his underwear. He moved swiftly to dress and head out the door, grabbing his backpack for good measure.

CHAPTER TWENTY-FIVE

Declan rounded the bend at a sharp clip, only to stop abruptly as Alexandria came down the trail. Countless stars scattered across the deep black sky like diamonds on velvet providing just enough light to see the path.

"Good timing." She smiled and indicated the trail with a nod of her head. "Let's go."

"Where? Didn't we do this tour once?"

She smiled. "Not this one."

The pace she set made him realize how leisurely the hike had been on Christmas Day. It seemed only a few minutes passed before they reached the high bluff, but she continued past the strewn rocks to where the fast trail led into the jungle. Alexandria paused, one hand on the trunk of the large breadfruit tree that marked the end of the trail, adjacent to the cliff edge.

She smiled seductively over her shoulder at him and stepped behind the trunk, disappearing from view. He followed and swept around the trunk, expecting to face her, but she wasn't there. His stomach lurched, but before he could freak out, a hand grabbed his ankle and her face appeared by the cliff edge.

"Down here, big fella."

Her impish smile made it impossible for him to snap at her.

She pointed with her left hand to natural handholds he had not seen and he climbed down beside her onto a narrow ledge that jutted out from the cliffside. Using roots sticking out of the soil and more handholds carved into the granite, he followed her along the ledge which appeared to curve into the cliff itself.

Alexandria ducked her head and swung around the bend, disappearing from view again.

Following Declan discovered the ledge curved in sharply along a worn, narrow trail that undercut the steep bluffs. It angled down and eventually terminated in a large cavern formed by the constant force of the ocean's tides. The semi-circular cavern was like an amphitheater facing the wide Pacific Ocean.

While he worked his way down to the ground level, he paused occasionally to appreciate the spectacle. The pre-dawn light didn't illuminate the whole cave, and spectral pools of darkness seemed to ebb and flow at what appeared to be the back of the cave. Large rocks from times gone by looked like dice tossed randomly on a soft, sandy stage.

Alexandria opened her backpack and pulled out a light-weight beach blanket and some containers. She set the containers on a large stone and spread the blanket nearby.

Moving to center stage, she motioned for him to join her among the large rocks and driftwood acting as well-placed props on the white, silken sand brushed clean by the receding tides. Declan slipped his backpack off and dropped it near the blanket. He paused before he moved to join her.

She stood facing the open sea.

He took a moment to appreciate her silhouette. Somewhere in the last few minutes, she had kicked off her hiking sandals and was wiggling her toes in the sand. On closer inspection, he found she was not wearing hiking gear but tan shorts riding low on her hips that stopped a couple of inches below her nicely shaped ass. Her trail shirt was unbuttoned and covered a barely-there undershirt.

He glided up beside her, and she slipped her hand into his, never turning her face from the open sea. The sound of waves breaking on the outer rocks echoed against the grotto walls behind them.

She glanced sidelong at him.

"You said you liked a good sunrise." Softly spoken words tickled his ears.

On the distant horizon, a warm glow erupted, pushing up against the dark night sky, forcing the stars into retreat while black gave way to ever-lightening shades of purple. A new moon was barely visible but faded fast before the onslaught of the rising sun. Golden rays broke through purple-gray cloud cover like beacons of hope.

Declan felt no need to speak but tightened his hold on her hand. He had seen majestic beauty like this play out before, but he had never felt so connected to it. The warmth of her hand in his was a lifeline—compassion, serenity, and peace flowed through him, undercut with an electric energy that made him ultra-aware of everything around him. Her nearness aroused him, and his body twitched in response to her unspoken call. The jasmine and sunshine scent of her skin on the salty dawn breeze intoxicated him.

He pulled his arm up and over her, stepping behind her,

pressing their clasped hands to her midriff, pulling her against his chest. Her hair was back in a loose ponytail, and he dipped his head to press his lips to the side of her throat. From his vantage point he could see her breasts rise and fall, her deep cleavage apparently unencumbered by a bra. *So hot.*

He tried to think logically. He needed to pull back before it was too late. "Al, this is too much. You deserve more than I can offer. I don't know if I can stop before things go too far," he whispered in her ear.

She dropped his hand and turned in his arms to face him.

Her gaze held him mesmerized as her hands slid up and over his chest, leaving a trail of tingling gooseflesh in their wake. His dick twitched in time to his rapidly increasing heartbeat.

Her gaze was intent and focused. "Declan, I belong to no one but me. My choices are my own. I am here with you because I choose to be. I want you, and..."

Before she could finish the sentence, he leaned into her, his hand cupping her neck, his thumb rubbing her jawline while his fingertips caressed the back of her neck, teasing her hairline. His mouth slanted across hers, warm, alive, and electric. His hands slid down under the collar of her trail shirt, and her arms dropped back for the few moments it took to push it down and off completely, letting it fall to the sandy beach.

The ever-present, low-level electric current between them exploded into liquid lightning, flowing through his veins with every beat of his heart. His cock was like a steel rod in his shorts and he shifted to provide a little extra room. Her mouth opened under his, her tongue meeting his eagerly. Her right hand slid up and over his shoulder to tangle in his hair, pulling him closer while the other glided down his chest and around to his back, her fingertips and nails tugging him closer. A guttural moan from deep in his abdomen exploded from him. In one swift move, Declan swept her up against his chest and, in a few long strides, he was at the blanket. He held her tight against his body as he laid her on the blanket, his torso half covering her, his mouth never breaking its connection. A hunger so deep he couldn't contain it broke loose. He trailed kisses along her jawline to her ear, his teeth taking the tender lobe in a soft bite.

Declan's warm breath in her ear sent shivers of exquisite delight along Alexandria's spine, igniting the liquid fire in her veins. The desire that had pooled in her womb the last several days erupted, and she felt the heat and wetness spread. Passion flooded her senses like a drug, and she wanted Declan's warm, naked skin pressed against her. She ached to have him deep within her. His lips left a trail of heat where they passed. His left hand caressed her, gliding down her throat to sweep his warm palm around her breast. Her breasts were swollen and tight, her nipples stiffening to peaks. When he pulled the soft cotton fabric of the shelf bra down and moved his mouth to suckle her breast, her hips pressed up against him.

He rolled the tender peak between his lips,

She shuddered under him.

He pulled back. His eyes dark with passion. "I want to watch you," he murmured.

A throaty laugh bubbled from her. "I'm right here, not

goin' anywhere." Her hands drifted over his body, savoring the warmth of his skin and marveling at the strength of him.

His hand glided down her body to her knee and back up, caressing and massaging her thigh. Her legs opened to him.

His fingers slid under the leg of her shorts, and he looked at her. "My, my."

She shrugged. "Underwear seemed like overkill this morning."

He laughed and ran his fingers through the curls of her mound.

She inhaled sharply.

Declan smiled wickedly and slid his thumb between her wet folds, rubbing her clit.

She threw her head back and moaning, pulling him closer.

He dipped his head to nuzzle her breast. "You're far too overdressed for my purposes," he murmured.

Popping the snap on her shorts, he had them unzipped before she could reply.

She lifted her hips and he pulled them down past her knees, slipping them off completely when she lifted her feet, then tossed them aside.

He rolled to his knees, taking her with him. One hand kneaded her ass cheek as he pulled her tight against him, pressing his hard-on firmly against her abdomen.

Alexandria moaned into his kiss, inflaming his senses beyond reason. He grabbed the hemline of her shirt, pulling it up and off, breaking his kiss only long enough to get the offending fabric out of the way. At the sight of her kneeling naked before him, her hair tumbling around her shoulders, the clip long since having fallen from her hair, his heart tightened. Her breasts rose and fell with each breath, teasing him to catch them in his mouth. He admired every inch of her, savoring the sight and his gaze rose to her face. She was biting her lip, self-doubt clouding her eyes.

Tilting her chin, he looked into her emerald eyes. "You are so beautiful."

She smiled wickedly. "I'd return the compliment, but you've got too many clothes on." Her hands began to pull his shirt up.

Happy to oblige, he reached up and behind him to grab a fistful of shirt and yanked it off, tossing it away. He brushed her hands aside and undid his shorts in a rush, standing to shove them down and kick them away before kneeling in front of her. He took her hands in his and spread her arms wide, watching her face as her gaze washed over him like a caress, lingering on his swollen cock. Her tongue ran across her upper lip.

He could stand no more, imagining her tongue on his hot flesh. Releasing her hands, he pulled her close. Sliding his hands down her back, he cupped her ass cheeks, squeezing them before moving his hands farther down her butt. Pulling her legs apart and over his, he sat back on his heels. Her mound pressed against the heat of his cock and he crushed her to him, the tight buds of her nipples hard against his chest. Her mouth against his, their tongues danced in tune with their heartbeats. He could almost swear too many hands involved, every inch of him tingled in awareness and every stroke of her hand left him wanting more of her.

Leaning forward, he laid her on her back. He kissed her

deeply before sliding down to her breasts, kneading, kissing, and sucking from one to the other.

Her hands tangled in his hair, pulling him tighter against her as her hips writhed beneath him.

Taking one of her hands, he put it to her own breast, his cock nearly ready to explode at the sight of her hand pressing and squeezing herself. Watching, he slid farther down her body, kissing her ribs and trailing his tongue around her naval.

Stroking up through the curls between her legs, her scent perfumed the salty air. His hot breath whispered against her skin. He continued to slide down until his face was between her thighs and he pressed her thighs up and apart until she placed her heels on his back. Feeling her shudder, he looked up to find her watching him, uncertainty in her eyes.

"You are beautiful everywhere, Alexandria." He lowered his mouth, his hot tongue sweeping up slowly from the bottom of her opening, tasting the honey of her essence, up and over her clit, sucking gently.

At the touch of Declan's tongue, Alexandria nearly came off the blanket. Feverish need consumed her as he lapped at her, sliding first one then two fingers inside her. His mouth worked her to an explosive pitch. She dug her heels into his back, spreading her knees ever wider to give him access, her chest heaving and deep guttural moans escaping her. One hand massaged her breasts and her other tangled in his hair, pulling him closer and urging him on, to bring her to orgasm. He worked her hard, and she felt herself contract deeply before exploding outward, his name a scream bursting from her as her climax hit. The rhythmic release of tension throughout her body arching her off the ground. Before she was fully flat on the ground, Declan was moving up her body, kissing and stroking the fires to an even higher pitch, and Alexandria was aware that a place deep inside her ached with need. A desire to be filled. She pulled him close.

Declan braced himself on one forearm, his other hand rubbing the head of his cock against the hot moist flesh of her womanhood.

Alexandria's legs were wrapped loosely around his hips.

He kissed her deeply and pushed in slightly, expanding her, then out. Only to enter again, a little deeper, lubricating himself with her fluids. He didn't want to hurt her and her sheath clung to him tightly, both welcoming and shunning his presence. He stared into her eyes, never breaking contact.

She licked her lips. "Declan, please..."

His resolve broke and he sheathed himself deeply.

Her eyes went wide.

He froze. *Holy shit.* He kissed away the tears forming at the corner of her eyes and mumbled words he wasn't even aware of to her. She pressed her hips tighter against him and he slowly started to withdraw only to have her tighten her legs around him.

"Don't," she murmured. She kissed his neck.

His last hesitation dissolved. "Relax, I'm not going anywhere," he whispered in her ear. Feeling the muscles in her legs soften, he withdrew slightly only to press back in slowly, filling and stretching her.

After a few moments, as his strokes grew stronger and longer, she started to respond to the rhythm.

He rose to his knees and lifted her hips to control his angle of penetration.

As her breathing deepened the sensations rocking her body, her eyes never left his face. Suddenly, she threw her head back and guttural cries of pleasure filled the cave.

Declan increased his tempo and as her name ripped from his lips, he pulled out quickly to spill himself on her stomach. He leaned forward, bracing himself on his forearms, and rested his forehead against hers, eyes closed, waiting for his breathing to return to normal. After a few moments he lifted himself off her, rolling her to her side and pulling her close in a spooning position.

She seemed unusually quiet and he wondered if she regretted her decision. He pulled the backpack over and rested his head on it since she was using his bicep as a pillow. He flipped the blanket behind him over his body to cover them both and held her quietly, waiting.

"Are you angry?"

When the words finally came, he was shocked. It took Declan a moment to answer. "Angry? Why would I be angry?"

Her voice was soft. "You pulled out so quickly. I don't have any experience. I didn't know what to do to make it better for you."

Declan turned her to face him. "Look at me." Green eyes met blue-gray. "I pulled out 'cause I figured, since you were a virgin, you weren't on birth control. You're amazing, and if I was upset with anything, it would be that you gave such a precious gift to a guy like me."

She smiled sweetly. "A guy like you. You mean a

womanizing playboy who, at every turn, has protected and watched over me? You mean that guy?"

Before he could respond, she rolled out of his arms and onto her feet.

He sat up and watched her walk to the water, appreciating the sway of her hips and the curve of her breasts.

She glanced at him over her shoulder. "I may have been a virgin, but I'm not naive. I spend the bulk of my time in places where anything could go wrong, and I wouldn't want an innocent to pay the price. I've been on birth control for years."

Tidal flow was ebbing, warm waters slipping and sliding around the nearby rocks. Farther from the sheltered cave, waves broke on large, jumbled rock formations scattered here and there, creating an almost natural breakwater for the inner pools.

He watched as the sand fell away under her feet and the water deepened around her. Getting to his feet, he followed her. When she started to dip down into the water he grabbed her up and spun her around. Time seemed to stand still as Declan gazed into her eyes, searching for what, he didn't know. He lowered his lips to hers, his tongue teasing the edge of her mouth, sliding across the sensitive surface before dipping inside to tango with her tongue.

As they parted, his hand splashed water onto her abdomen and he carefully washed away the evidence of his orgasm. He smiled. "Never let it be said, I don't clean up after myself."

She laughed heartily and, in a swift unanticipated move, she knocked his legs out from under him, dunking him in the sea only to dive in on top of him.

CHAPTER TWENTY-SIX

The late afternoon sun reflected off the crystal vase of tropical flowers Margaret had left on the dining table, creating prisms of rainbow light that danced on the walls. Alexandria grinned at the dust motes frolicking in their beams. As she cleared the end of the hallway, she heard voices from just inside the home theatre. She paused, reluctant to intrude. Recognizing Louisa's sultry voice, she started to turn back when the words froze her in her tracks.

"Come on, Declan, you can't imagine in your wildest dreams that that young thing can compare to me in any way when it comes to love? And stop fooling yourself, honey, you know I'm in your thoughts all the time."

Alexandria cocked her head, waiting for Declan to decry her claims.

A momentary silence was broken by his voice, strong and sure. "Louisa, you're right on both counts. She can't compete with you, and damn it, you have been in my thoughts all this time."

As the words sliced through her heart, Alexandria crushed her fist to her mouth to keep from crying out. She whirled and ran down the hall, as quiet and quick as a mouse eluding a hunting cat.

Declan shook his head and snorted. He looked around the theatre room and then back at Louisa. His gaze raked her from top to bottom.

Smiling, she ran her tongue across her full lower lip and slid her hands down her hips.

"How could I have ever thought that I loved you?" Contempt so strong he wanted to vomit rocked him.

Disbelief washed across her face.

"You're right. Alexandria could never be compared to you. You're a cold, heartless bitch who would do anything and use anyone to achieve what you want. You have no ethics and no morals. All you have is a shell, and even your shell isn't that great. My greatest shame is that I've allowed you to darken my thoughts and impact my life all this time. What a waste of my energy and my life. Alexandria is sweet and kind, beautiful and passionate. You couldn't begin to understand those traits. Not to mention the love she has for her family or the sacrifices she would make to protect those she loves. The fact that I wasted so much time thinking I was broken-hearted over you instead of being relieved that I escaped being saddled with such a heartless bitch is repre-hensible."

The wide-eyed, slack-jawed look on Louisa's face was priceless. He walked away, but paused at the door and looked over his shoulder. "Louisa, don't ever speak to me again. You're the past and so far in it, I don't even want to think about it. Get your things and get off this island. Today.

Stay the hell out of my way and out of my life, or I'll make yours miserable."

As Alexandria whirled to flee from the great room, she saw Edin and Meredith deep in conversation by the pool and a group of people at the trail head. She fled along the corridor of the family wing to the exit door at the end of the hall. Instead of heading down island toward the sunny beach, she turned to the dark jungle trail heading up the island. Alexandria ran along the narrow path to where a sharp turn around a giant rock face breached the jungle edge. She pressed against the rock-face and slid down to a crumpled mess at the base.

Anguish knifed through her and her arms curled around her mid-section. How could she have been so stupid? She knew better. She did. Hadn't she learned her lesson with Brent? Hadn't Edin, Dad, and even Brent and that bitch Louisa warned her? For that matter, Declan himself had warned her.

Tears of anguish coursed down her face. She should have known better. After Brent, she had thought she lost her chance at love. What a fool! What did she know of love? She'd run away and allowed herself to be bitter and wounded, determined never to be involved with another guy.

Sobs racked her shoulders and her muscles tightened to the point of pain. *If I had known how much real love did hurt, I would...* She sat up straighter and as her sobs began to subside, hiccupped. *What would I have done? I didn't even know what love was until I met Declan. I never was this worked up over Brent, even after I caught him with his lover.*

She focused on breathing deep and slow and, although tears continued to slide down her cheeks unheeded, her jumbled thoughts began to jell. A fist tightened around her heart at the thought of how easily he had dismissed making love with her that very morning. But, then again, he probably didn't think of it as more than an easy lay from just another conquest. What an ass! Brent was right, Declan was no better than him, just more politic about it. Even as her logic solidified her case against him, a small voice kept whispering, *"What if you're wrong?"* She determinedly ignored it.

If she was honest, this was exactly what she had asked Dad and Edin to let her do. Fail. Fall on her face. If she wasn't flat on her face now, she didn't know what would qualify.

Her hands dirty from the ground, she used the hem of her shirt to wipe away the tracks of her tears. Somehow, she had buck up and get through this. The island was too small to get lost on and she couldn't get off it without hurting the ones she loved. And she didn't want to run this time. If their time together meant so little to Declan, that was on him. But even with her shattered heart, she'd stand tall for Edin and Meredith.

She made her way back down the trail to the backdoor by her apartment. Fortunately, there were other people on the island and she could avoid any private moments with Declan. The last thing she needed was to be called out on her stupidity.

Seeing Edin talking to Declan at the end of the long hall she slipped noiselessly into her room. She had spent enough time around wild animals to know how to slip past one.

CHAPTER TWENTY-SEVEN

"E, we need to find a way." Declan was ready to shake Edin into compliance, and his friend's lack of enthusiasm was pissing him off.

"In theory, I agree, but how do we manage this?"

Edin's logical approach to problem solving was getting in the way of Declan's very emotional desire to get Louisa off the island and cut short her ball-busting schemes.

Over Edin's shoulder, Declan caught a brief glimpse of a disheveled Al slipping into her room.

Edin gave him a weird look and glanced back over his shoulder at the now-empty hallway. "What?" he asked.

Declan shook his head. "Nothing, must have been a strange shadow."

The look on Edin's face said he wasn't taking the bait, but Declan didn't want to enlighten him. He'd figure that out on his own.

Declan flashed a big smile. "Let's find the guys. There has to be enough brainpower between us to short circuit one vicious bitch."

Declan's frustration was growing exponentially. They hadn't heard back from Tom's brother-in-law, a Chicago PD detective with connections to a private investigator that he thought could help them.

Alexandria had studiously avoided him at dinner and throughout the evening. Every time he tried to get near her to talk, she engaged some other member of the group and then had disappeared altogether.

Watching Louisa's shit-eating grin grow as the evening unfolded just made his mood fouler. He wanted nothing more than to see her off the island. She seemed to be taking his earlier dictates way too calmly and that set his nerves on edge. She wasn't one to let anything slide.

The slightest thought of Alexandria made his dick jump to attention and hiding the constant wood in his shorts was tough as hell. Not to mention, he had no idea where they would go from here. He hadn't had a relationship since—well, shit—he'd never had one. He couldn't, wouldn't, count the twisted, sick thing he'd had with Louisa as a relationship. How the fuck could he discuss anything with Al when he couldn't even figure out what he wanted? Edin and John were watching him like he was a rabid, caged tiger. So much for a restful, relaxing holiday.

He glanced skyward. Brilliant stars littered the sky, and the patio lights held the darkness at bay around the pool. The faint smell of a wood fire tickled the back of his mind. Music playing in the background made him want to dance. *Where the fuck did that thought come from?* He shook his head to clear it. Where all these pansy-ass thoughts were coming from, he just couldn't tell, but the thought of Al pressed up tight against him as they swayed to music persisted.

He stood and headed for the bar.

Rudy grinned in greeting but, before he could speak, one of the dock hands leapt from the darkness onto the pool deck.

"Fire! There's a fire in the supply warehouse!" He turned to head back to the beach with John and Edin hot on his heels.

Without pause, Declan, as well as the rest of the pool deck population, charged down the trail.

When he cleared the trees at the end of the trail, he was at a dead run. Clouds of black smoke were choking the beach before billowing upward. The small warehouse where he and Alexandria had found the Christmas ornaments was fully involved. An orange wall of flames climbed up the side of the wall containing the doors.

Dozens of deck hands and island workers had formed a bucket brigade, but progress was slow. Someone handed him a bucket, but instead of moving into the line, Declan glanced around for Edin and John.

John was helping a group of guys wrestle a portable water gun into position.

Edin was at the closest dock, pulling dry standpipe hose free to stretch from the end of the dock to the pumping equipment.

Declan started toward Edin but slid to a stop. He turned and searched the crowd for a familiar red-head. Nothing. Margaret and the other women were passing buckets in the brigade. Fear sluiced along his spine and he did a slow one-eighty, searching for Louisa.

Edin called his name, and he looked across the beach to him. He held up his hand to acknowledge him, but he turned back to look at the blazing fire. His intuition turned his face north to the cliffs, and he followed it like magnetic north. His heart jackhammering in his chest, Declan dropped his bucket and sprinted for the main trail.

———

Sitting on the big, flat stone near the cliff edge, with the night sky spread out in a panorama of black velvet and diamond brightness, Alexandria pulled her knees up to her chest and wrapped her arms around them. The faint smell of wood smoke caught her attention, and she was glad she had escaped the pool deck. A beach bonfire would be a tough place to avoid Declan. She reached for the water bottle in her backpack.

"Well, well, well. What do we have here? Playing a little hard to get?"

Louisa's sarcastic tone caused Alexandria to whip around in surprise. "What are you doing here?" Alexandria came to her feet, wary.

Louisa was still at the edge of the jungle, hidden in shadows.

"I came for you." Louisa's evil grin leered in the stark white starlight as she stepped out from the shadows. In her right hand, a 9 mm Beretta pointed at Alexandria. She gestured with the gun. "It's amazing what you can pack in your checked bag if you disassemble it. Lucky for me...not so much for you."

Fear a cold pit in her stomach, Alexandria swallowed hard. Animal predators she could understand—the need to survive, to eat, drove them. But she was out of her element faced with a bat-shit crazy blonde. *Keep her busy, it works on TV shows.*

"What do you want?"

"I want you to die. I mean, I'm sorry, chicklet, but that's the only way my plan will work. Declan will be mine, well, at least for a while, and then when he dies," she gave a little laugh, "I'll have control of the company." She smiled. "Of course, he will be a tragic accident, not like your suicide."

"My suicide? I'm not killing myself, not over him and not for you." Alexandria's spine stiffened with anger. Her backpack was behind her. And a banana and a water bottle weren't much use against a Beretta.

Louisa rolled her eyes. "Good grief, it's not like you have a choice, really. Here's how it's going down. You're going over the cliff." She gestured toward the cliff with the gun, while she used her left to pull a small envelope from the back pocket of her shorts. "I'm going to leave this lovely little suicide note that I forged in your handwriting in your backpack there. Neat and tidy all around, wouldn't you say?"

"Hardly, since I'm not cooperating. You're going to have to shoot me." The jungle was too far to make a run for it.

Shrill, cold laughter echoed in the night, and Louisa pressed the envelope against her chest in an exaggerated sense of drama. "Oh, you are so innocent. Let me put it this way. If you don't go over the cliff on your own, I'll shoot you and leave you on the cliff edge. I'll march back down the trail and put a bullet in the brain pan of every member of your family, come back up here, put the gun in your hand, and voila--you are the psycho daughter who came back into the family fold only to lose it and kill everyone and yourself."

Fear for her family had Alexandria hanging her head, searching for an out but knowing she would do exactly as Louisa asked to protect them. "I don't understand why you would do this."

"Of course, you don't. Declan won't cooperate and take me back. The little business about his 'suicidal' lover in Chicago didn't do the trick, but if a number two goes down the tubes, he'll need an alibi. Someone who will fill the gaps and keep the media at a distance. I'll fill the role nicely." She snorted. "You practically wrote the script for this play-out. The unstable, missing-in-action sister, rejected in love. Brent planted the seeds, and you fertilized them with your insecurities. Of course, he won't be getting you out of the bargain, but he is of little consequence."

Louisa laughed again and reached down to shove the note into the outer net pocket of the backpack. "It's all just business, dear, a little complicated for a twit like you. Although, I have to say you gave me more competition than I bargained for. Who would have thought he'd fall for you?"

Alexandria's head snapped up. "What?"

"Oh, this is rich. You're not playing hard to get—come chase me. You're mooning."

"I heard him agree that I couldn't compete with you."

"Well, thank God you didn't hang around for the whole conversation or I would have had to force your sorry ass up here instead of just following you."

The whine in her voice rose, and her eyes flashed. "He championed you like a slobbering, lovesick puppy. Disgusting! You wouldn't know the first thing about how to handle a man! I've been using my assets since I was twelve to get what I need." She used her free hand to caress her breast and then slide down to rub her crotch.

Bile rose in Alexandria's throat and her hand rose to her throat to press back the urge to vomit. *She is fucking crazy.*

Louisa stepped closer, an arm's length away, and gestured with the gun. "It's time. Move your ass."

Alexandria glanced over the cliff side and made her

choice. "There's a ledge just below. That's not going to work. It has to be more in the middle." She stepped closer to Louisa who eyed her warily.

"Louisa!" As Declan burst from the trail head his yell erupted.

Louisa swung the gun toward him.

Alexandria reacted. She surged forward, adrenaline giving her added impetus, and hit Louisa's gun arm, making the shot go wild. Al brought her knee up hard into Louisa's abdomen and, as the blonde doubled over, she pumped her leg hard and brought her knee up into Louisa's face.

Louisa jerked upright.

Al stayed with her, her left hand grabbing Louisa's gun hand, fighting to keep the gun pointed away. Both women fell back toward the cliff edge. Louisa's left hand clawed at Alexandria, who was focused on the gun hand. She slammed Louisa's hand hard against the rocks, but Louisa kept her grip on the gun.

Alexandria realized they were too close to the edge. She felt the small rubble sliding away beneath them and knew they going along, slipping over the edge. The upward rush of cool salty sea air and the absence of rock told her they were over.

Louisa screamed, her eyes wide, and she dropped the gun as she grabbed for non-existent handholds.

Alexandria released her grip and looked at the sea below.

A large hand grabbed her ankle while another grabbed the back of her shorts, and her descent jerked to a stop. She couldn't close her eyes, watching Louisa flail and scream until she slammed into the turbulent surf below.

Al pushed her hands against the stone cliff face and looked up and back over her shoulder. Half off the cliff,

Declan had her shorts and ankle in a death grip and was inching backward ever so slowly.

She tried to help by leveraging some of her weight on her hands, pushing back up. It felt like forever before her legs and hips were over the edge.

As she breached the top edge, she glanced over her shoulder to see Edin lying on the cliff top, holding on to Declan's calves as the three scooted back from the edge.

Declan pulled himself into a sitting position and hauled her into his lap.

The hoarseness of his voice cut through her fog of shock.

"Oh my God, oh my God." He pulled her close and kissed her, rocking her, rubbing her back and stroking her hair.

As she laid her head on his chest with his strong arms around her, she started to cry.

Tears coursed down Edin's face. He crawled on his knees to envelop them in a big bear hug, kissing them both on the forehead and rocking with them. "Holy shit, I thought I was going to lose you both."

Relaxing his hold enough for her to lean back and cup her brother's tear stained cheek, Declan wiped the tears from her eyes.

Declan managed a small, tense smile. "Buddy, I just found her. I'm not losing her now."

He turned back to Alexandria and rubbed his thumb along her jawline before turning her face to his for a soft, gentle kiss.

CHAPTER TWENTY-EIGHT

The great room and pool deck had been transformed into what seemed like a central operations center. John and Edin entered the great room where friends and family gathered after the night's events, while the authorities from Saipan congregated on the deck.

Margaret rushed to her husband's side.

He slid his arm around her and kissed her temple.

Edin went to Meredith, sitting beside her on the couch and pulling her close.

John cleared his throat. "Well, things are pretty well wrapped up. The Ports Authority police will finish their investigation, but they are confident they have their man. Or should I say their woman?"

Alexandria shuddered. "I can't believe she survived that fall."

John shook his head. "The medivac team said she's barely hanging on. Her face took quite a pounding and most of her large bones are broken." He paused, pressing his lips together. "I know it sounds heartless, but I wish she hadn't."

His voice wavered, and he looked at Alexandria, curled

in the protection of Declan's arms on the oversized chaise. "When I think of what she tried to do." His gaze went to Declan. "As a businessman, I can thank you any way you choose. As a father, I could never thank you enough."

Declan nodded and smiled. "No thanks needed, John. Your blessing is more than enough."

John looked to his daughter. Her soft smile and healthy glow, sans the scraps and abrasions she wore, was vibrant and full of life. Thanks to the man holding her. But there was something more. As he stared at her, he saw the love in her eyes and realized she had made her choice and chosen wisely. He looked back to Declan and nodded his blessing.

"Hey. What about me? They would have both slid over the cliff if I hadn't grabbed him." Edin wasn't to be outdone.

Meredith playfully smacked him. "Isn't it enough that you're my hero every hour of every day?"

Rudy leaned forward. "About that, exactly how the hell did you two figure out what was going on?"

Declan shrugged. "I don't know. My mother used to preach to me about following my intuition. Man, when we hit that beach, my intuition was screaming at me to find Al. I didn't see her there, and I knew she wouldn't let the ladies have fun on the fire brigade without her. Suddenly, I just knew in my gut that she was at the cliffs, and she was in danger. I didn't know Edin was behind me."

Edin snorted. "I almost wasn't, but when I saw you drop that bucket and take off like a jackalope on steroids, well, I knew something big was wrong. The warehouse is just a room full of stuff. Besides, it was sprinklered on the inside, which meant that kind of fire had to be set. When you left, I knew I had to go, but I'm not as fast and was losing ground."

He choked. "Then I heard that gun shot, and I flew out of the trail head like I've never run before. I saw you diving for the cliff edge and I just knew you were going over and I pounced on you. Thank God you're so damn tall. I had just enough leverage to tip the balance."

John trembled as the realization of how close Alexandria and Declan had come to losing their lives quieted the room. Alexandria had already given her statements to the Ports Authority Police who arrived from Saipan after he'd called for Louisa's emergency evacuation.

John slid onto the loveseat and pulled Margaret down beside him. Although pale and shaken, she was a trooper in her own right.

Her gaze took in the room of friends and family. Some were covered in soot or smoke stained. Some were scrapped and bruised, but all alive and well. "Well, thank Heaven you're all safe and sound. We have an extra special reason to celebrate New Year's Eve tonight, but I think in the meantime, everyone should try to get some rest."

Lunch was quiet. And early—more of a brunch. Alexandria smiled. By general consensus, everyone decided to just clean up and regroup. Too wound up to sleep, they just wanted to be together.

She was good with that. Nestled next to Declan on the love seat, she wasn't really hungry and preferred to sip her hot toddy, courtesy of Margaret.

Tom entered with Rosamund from the guest wing. "Sorry we're late. I was talking to my partner in Chicago." Tom's step was sure and decisive as the two of them settled on the loveseat across from her.

"Louisa's insanity runs much deeper than anyone realized."

Tom's tone captured the attention of the room.

He looked to Victor. "The woman your brother hooked up with is none other than Louisa's younger sister, Charlene. She was apprehended yesterday trying to kill your sister-in-law, Meghan."

Victor paled considerably and swallowed hard. "I think I need a whiskey."

"Sorry, at ten in the morning, coffee will have to do." Margaret shoved a hot mug into Victor's trembling hands.

Tom accepted a mug of coffee as well. "Charlene doesn't have Louisa's expertise, and she cracked under interrogation. They planned for Meghan to die and for Charlene to marry your brother after a respectable time. Apparently, your brother's affair isn't the only mischief he's been up to, and Charlene has dirt on him that had him at her beck and call."

He jutted his chin at Victor. "I'll give you all the details later."

"But why did she come here?" At the memory of Louisa's wide-eyed rant on the cliff, Alexandria shuddered, and Declan tightened his arm around her.

Tom frowned. "Charlene was waiting for word from Louisa. Declan's been less manipulatable than her usual mark and, despite warnings from Charlene, he's been the golden prize she wouldn't walk away from. She's had him under surveillance for months and was getting desperate. Hence the blending of the two marks to get her here. Louisa figured if she had a way to drive him to her, for media protection, alibi, or something, she could get him to marry her. As the only heir to Ruaidhrí Pharma, she intended to eliminate him down the road and take possession of his family business."

Alexandria shook her head. "That's what she said at the cliffs."

Rosamund nudged Tom's arm and he continued. "Charlene and Louisa suicided the girl in Chicago and pointed the media at Declan."

Declan closed his eyes and shook his head. "Poor Miriam. It's my fault after all."

"Don't go there, man."

The authority in Tom's voice made Alexandria turn away from Declan to stare at him.

"When I say Charlene cracked, she cracked hard. She and Louisa have been black widowing marks for over fifteen years. She confessed that they ran similar situations in Los Angeles, New York, and Miami. A change of scenery, a change of name, and they started again. Charlene thought they were done with you years ago. Seems Louisa was getting cocky and trying to run two marks at once. You caught her with your competitor from Miami and escaped the game. He didn't. He married a voluptuous younger woman six months after that incident and died eighteen months later."

Alexandria snuggled even closer to Declan.

Tom took a swig of coffee. "Somewhere along their developmental path, somebody fucked those two up royally."

John shook his head in wonder before turning to Tom. "Your partner is a software security engineer at a gaming firm and he found all this out?"

Tom's neck flushed.

Rosamund bumped him with her shoulder.

"Not exactly. The gaming firm is a cover. We both work for the FBI, and on occasion, Homeland Security. We tapped a few contacts to help us out."

With an info-bomb like that, the room erupted into curious questions about spies and intrigue that Alexandria was happy to tune out.

———

Cool, moist, early evening breezes rustled the pale, ivory silk sheers billowing away from the open window. The air smelled of rain after the tropical squall that had blown through in the afternoon.

Cuddled in the middle of her king-sized bed amidst linens strewn every which way, Alexandria nestled her cheek against Declan's chest and listened to the steady, soothing rhythm of his heartbeat. His arms tightened around her and he kissed the top of her head.

She turned her face toward his for a long, languid kiss. His tongue traced the outline of her lips and she shivered at the tickle of it. She smiled.

"Did I thank you for saving my life?"

He grinned. "What? Saved your life? I didn't save your life, I saved mine. Because I couldn't live in a world without you in it."

His eyes grew serious and she touched her fingertips to his chin.

He stroked her cheek softly. "I was a fool before I met you. I had no clue what love was or how lonely and empty my life had become."

She started to speak but when his index finger softly shushed her lips, held her peace.

"When I was a kid, I used to daydream about the day I would have a family and we would open presents by the Christmas tree and count our blessings. But then my mom died and my dad was never the same. I swore I'd never love like that. My dreams faded, and I lost sight of things. I thought I knew all I needed to know, then you walked into my life and tossed me on my ass. Everything I thought I knew went right out the window."

Her hand stroked his chest, and gooseflesh rose in its wake. She pressed a kiss to his heart. "I was so angry when my mother died that I stopped moving forward, at least, emotionally. I lost faith—Dad and Edin were more right than I wanted to admit. I was stuck in the past." She looked into Declan's eyes. "But now, you've given me the greatest Christmas present I could ever imagine. You've given me the present—and love for a lifetime of Christmases ahead of us."

The End

DEAR READER

Without a dog and a boy, this book would never have been realized. The dog was my Irish Wolfhound, Handsome. The boy was my son, Evan, whom I should probably refer to as a man.

When my son, Evan, was preparing to leave for college, he told me I should write a book and he would go to university. We had often laughed over my crazy dreams. Once, he said, "Don't tell me you had a strange dream. Just tell me you had a dream. I'll know it was strange."

I laughed and recounted our conversation to my friend, Alexis Montgomery, whom I had met when *her* wolfhound puppy, Handsome, decided I was the love of his life. The feeling was mutual, by the way. Since we were fairly new friends at the time, I didn't realize she was a writer. She pounced on my story and invited me to a meeting of the Orange County Chapter of Romance Writers of America (OCC-RWA). And the rest, as they say, is history.

My family has always recognized my love of reading—it is legend amongst those who know me. I am the one who will be reading on the wine-tasting trip with friends, or at a party, or standing in Costco.

But today, you are the reader. My hope is that I have given you the journey you both expected and didn't expect. I hope you enjoyed *The Christmas Present* and I offer my heartfelt thanks for reading it. I hope to entertain you again soon.

ABOUT THE AUTHOR

Frances Amati writes fantasy/paranormal and contemporary romance. A member of the Orange County Chapter of Romance Writers of America, she has been a finalist twice in the prestigious Orange Rose Contest and three times in the California Dreaming Conference's Hooker Contest. Her first short story, *Heart Hound,* was published in the OCC-RWA Anthology *Romancing the Pages.*

A full time Senior Property Manager for a real estate services firm, this mother of three grown children and "Nonna" to five darling grandchildren, keeps her sanity with large doses of humor and frequent reality checks administered by her Irish Wolfhounds. Her family is close knit and inspires many of her characters.

Additional installments in the Holiday Hearts Series will release in mid-2020. Her fantasy/paranormal series will start releasing in early 2020. You can get to know her better at www.francesamati.com, where you can register for her newsletter, or find her on Facebook @FCAmati.

An avid traveler with various hobbies, Frances currently resides in Huntington Beach, California with her Irish Wolfhounds, who remind her that love is what we make it.

Made in the USA
San Bernardino, CA
13 December 2019

61403928R00120